# Katrin's Chronicles: The Canon of Jacquelene Dyanne, Vol. 1

Valerie C. Woods

Katrin's Chronicles: The Canon of Jacqueléne Dyanne, Vol. 1



Published by BooksEndependent LLC
**www.BooksEndependent.com**



Cover and Interior Design by
Jacqueline D. Woods/J.D. Woods Consulting

ISBN: 978-0-9887687-2-7

Also by Valerie C. Woods

*I Believe...*
*A Ghost Story for the Holidays*
(novella)

*Something For Everyone:*
*(Original Monologues for Women, for Men,*
*etc., etc.)*

# Table of Contents

# Dedication

*To Mom and Dad,*

*My elder siblings*

*And especially the sister who inspired such great adventures in our youth.*

# Initiation

August 7, 1971

The first year is the hardest. At least that's what Grand Anne says. I'd believe her if I were you. But then, you don't know my grandmother yet. Actually, I didn't know her as well as I thought. But in the past three years, I've gotten to know her extremely well.

In any case, the end of summer '68 initiated changes that continue to unfold to this day. It's vital that the events be fully chronicled. I mean, here we are three years down the road and the stories, rumors and outright fabrications concerning the adventures of Jacqueléne Dyanne DuBois, whom you will get to know very well, are too numerous and over-the-top to count.

I've known J. Dyanne my entire life. I was her companion on the many occasions when she accomplished her most amazing accomplishments. And more to the point, because of my experience reporting for the Nightingale Elementary Gazette, I've filled several composition books with notes of our activities. Therefore, it seems only fitting that it is I, Katrin the Youngest, who can justly tell the tale. And it's time.

In a few short weeks I begin another first-year experience. High School. So, Grand Anne gifted me with a typewriter for 8th grade graduation to formally document that other first year – 1968 – the year of our initiation into a legacy of infinite mystery.

To begin, let me clear up a few things.

J. Dyanne does not communicate with little moon aliens or Martians. She does not have a crystal ball, nor was she responsible for the outcome of the last presidential election. And she certainly does not command the dead. She may speak with them from time to time, but command them? Who can do that? What could you possibly use to exert pressure to obey? I mean they're already dead. Perhaps threaten them with life?

The idea that J. Dyanne is some kind of evil sorceress is, to my way of thinking, perfectly silly, regardless of what certain people who live around the corner might think.

And it's not fair to label me as abnormally different either. Just because I memorized the Gettysburg Address doesn't make me a genius. I mean, it is a memorable piece of writing. Besides, one of my many uncles bet me I couldn't. And the money I subsequently won came in handy. But I admit, I love the words. I mean, "Fourscore and seven years ago..." Sure, Lincoln could have said, "Eighty-seven years ago..." or "In 1776..." but the flow just isn't the same, you know? I confess I love words and language. They have, quite literally, changed my life. But that's another story.

Finally, contrary to popular belief, J. Dyanne does not know everything. This is not a slur – she'd say the same thing herself. However, let me also say that she does have an incisive, fiercely inquiring mind that grasps complex concepts with some degree of ease. It is this that gives those of lesser quickness the impression of omniscience.

For instance, many still believe that it was J. Dyanne who, in March 1968, prophesized the accident that resulted in the broken leg of one Derek Fremont, the then thirteen-year-old delinquent who lives three houses down. But what do you expect will happen when you ride backwards on the handlebars of a handmade, motorized bicycle? Even I could have predicted the result and I only possess the vision afforded by the glasses I have been forced to wear since the 4th grade.

Granted, the specificity with which J. Dyanne was able to identify the location, number and severity of the fractured bones, as well as the fact that it was indeed his right leg and not the left that was put in a cast, may have fueled the rumors of prophecy. But really, she's just very observant.

But at the time, people were prone to believe anything.

It was Chicago, August 1968, a time of extraordinary things, when the unbelievable turned out to be very believable after all. Therefore, I will, through these official chronicles, do my humble best to clarify the chaos and set the record straight. If I don't, who will?

As Grand Anne also says, if you don't write your

own history, someone else will make it up for you.

Although there are many instances of J. Dyanne's intellect and expanded awareness recounted among family and close friends, my goal here is to formally archive with as much accuracy as memory will allow, the true canon of Jacqueléne Dyanne – her life and work. So far.

I will return to the beginning. A time when I was a regular sixth grader, innocent of what I now know was a turning point. It all began on a fairly ordinary day on the South Side of Chicago in a neighborhood of modest homes and two-story apartment buildings, on tree-lined streets and fenced backyards. That day culminated in the first of a series of events to which the local press gave the fanciful title of "The Strange Case of the South Side Seer."

Nonsense, of course, but the media does like a fantastic story to feed the frenzy.

# Chapter 1 - Seventy-Five Forty-One

August 1968

It was in the waning days of summer, near the end of the period called "dog days." In ancient times, Sirius, the Dog Star, appeared in the heavens at sunrise, signaling the beginning of the hottest, muggiest days of the year. The ancients perceived it to be an evil time when dogs went mad, the seas churned to boiling point and men were prone to burning fevers. They used to sacrifice a brown dog to calm the raging Sirius, but the practice isn't so popular nowadays. Fortunately. But anything could happen during days like this. That's why I always carried high hopes for this time of year.

The air was saturated with anticipation. Something was going to happen. Something had to happen. It was time for that unknown, magic something that would make this a summer to remember. The thing maybe you'd write about or keep in your private memories forever. That's what I always hoped for August. It could be anything. Who knew today would be one of those "anything" days.

The morning sun shimmered into the rooms I shared with J. Dyanne at 7541 Winthrop Avenue. We slept in what we called "the sweatbox," the rooms at the top of the house. Heat rises, you know, and even with the slight breeze through the screened windows I could tell it would be another hot, muggy day. As usual. The only unusual thing I noticed was I had wakened first. J. Dyanne was an eager, early riser, never wishing to waste time sleeping when she had projects to complete.

Her sleep seemed restless, perhaps even troubled. Hot as it was, she was curled, cocooned in the thin cotton top sheet. I slipped out of the room and down to breakfast careful not to disturb her.

At 7541 it was imperative to wear shoes at all times. I was glad of the furry slippers one of the Aunts had given the previous Christmas. Now, in August they weren't as plush, and perfect for mornings. You see, a fine dust covered the floors due to the fact that the structure was in a constant state of renovation by the owners. Neither J. Dyanne nor I had any say in this matter, as the owners were, in fact, our parents. Since we could always blame the smudges and stains on our clothes to the state of the house rather than our own careless or clumsy behavior, it was a fair enough trade.

I was the youngest member to 7541 having arrived there eleven Aprils before. J. Dyanne was before me by almost two Octobers. The Elder Others, one male, the other female, had already gained years that ranged into the teens. Their physical presence was sporadic and often silent.

In the breakfast room, I opened the curtains to the window that looked out to the back porch and the yard beyond. *Pater familias* (yes, that's Latin for 'father of the family' – as a future doctor, it only makes sense to begin my studies now) was in the garage working on his motorcycle. The grass needed cutting so I hoped J. Dyanne woke soon so we could get out before anyone else noticed. I prepared cold cereal. The Teen Elder Others were either still sleeping or onto their own adventures. The faithful hound, Dog, joined me when he smelled the preparation for my second course of buttered toast and grape jelly. He sniffed, ever hopeful, under the table. J. Dyanne arrived just as I finished reading the comics in the *Chicago Sun-Times*.

"You were talking in your sleep again, Katrin," she stated. "Something about a sword." I watched as she prepared her own bowl of cereal and toast, carefully measuring out her portions. Precision and balance were very important to J. Dyanne, though the expression was sometimes inconsistent. For instance, food preparation was exact, but her dress code was often haphazard. To her, it was important to be healthy, but why waste valuable thinking on mere appearance? We definitely parted ways on that point. I thought about my appearance quite a lot. Well, at least compared to J. Dyanne.

"Very distracting," she continued. "Reading the Merlin stuff, I suppose." I was, but how did she know? Again, here was an example of J. Dyanne's uncanny ability to draw solid conclusions with a minimum of information. Sometimes it felt like she could even read my mind, but of course that was nonsense. Or so I believed at the time. Settling down with her meal and the sports section, she laid out the day's plan.

"Today, we'll shift our focus. The librarian at Hamilton Park promised me a new book on the early Dutch painters. We'll walk. It clears the mind." And then she dived into her food and the *Sun-Times*.

Why J. Dyanne would need her mind cleared I didn't then know. Or perhaps she meant mine. I studied her profile. She had high cheekbones and a strong jaw line, which often led people who didn't know her well to believe she was unyielding. But these were the same people who had never seen her face soften with laughter and reveal the dimple on her right cheek. The restless night didn't show on her face. She seemed her usual alert self and ready for the day's excursion.

Usually a summer day would find us either playing softball or watching a baseball game on television. The Chicago Cubs had just finished a five game winning streak against the Atlanta Braves and were heading to Houston. Don't ask me why, as South Siders, we weren't White Sox fans, but there it is. It may have had something to do with the ivy-covered walls of the outfield at the Cubs' North Side ballpark. As first baseman Ernie Banks often said, they were the "friendly confines of Wrigley Field." In any case, since there was no game to watch that day, we could spend as much time as we wanted on our adventure. The proposed hike to the local library combined exercise for the body and the mind. It was likely to be at least 90 degrees again, and hopefully, the air conditioner was working at the park's field house library.

We had once visited the Central Library downtown in The Loop, along with our grandmother, the aforementioned Grand Anne. Compared to the local library, this place was immense and extraordinary with marble staircases, mosaics, stained class and, of course, tons of books. It was like some ancient sacred space to which we'd made a solemn pilgrimage.

Between them, Grand Anne and Mom were responsible for our reading habits. Birthday presents were often subscriptions to a new book club or renewal of *Children's Highlights* magazine. We were never refused library privileges. And when we were young, Mom would read to us every night.

Though many in our peer group did not understand our passion for reading, J. Dyanne and I often set out early, like today, to return the four or five books we'd read during the previous two weeks and select new ones. The Central Library was a complicated journey via bus and L train. We looked forward to the completion of the new Lake-Dan Ryan train, which would be walking distance from the house and make travel to The Loop a breeze. But even if the new L had been finished, now was not the time to try it on our own.

The city was pretty much under siege because 'Da Mare' – that would be the honorable mayor Richard J. Daley – was preparing to welcome the nation's Democrats. A bunch of demonstrators protesting the Vietnam War, promoting civil rights and Black Power, you name it, were all coming to town as well. This made the police more than usually, well, irritable. So the mayor was also preparing a welcome for the demonstrators: The National Guard. And he said they could shoot to kill. If necessary.

Things being what they were, seeking adventure close to home seemed like a promising enterprise to me. Besides, the parents had decreed that we could exercise our black power in the relative safety of our own neighborhood.

J. Dyanne was already clothed. She had chosen to adorn her athletic frame with the usual Keds, ankle socks, shorts and shirt and one of her many caps. This told me that the day could turn very active. I quickly consumed my remaining toast and left the room to dress for the day. Despite the heat, I wore yellow pedal pushers with my Keds and ankle socks, topped with a white, sleeveless blouse. And although it took J. Dyanne less than five minutes to get ready, thanks to her expedient use of hats, I required more time, thanks to the struggle with my hair. Once straightened, my hair was thin and hard to control. The bangs were fine, most of the time, but if I wore it loose, it never stayed in place. The best option was to confine it into two pigtails with rubber bands. By the end of the day, they were usually sticking straight out the back like wings, so I looked like I was in a perpetual high wind. But that couldn't be helped.

"Leave a note," J. Dyanne advised upon my return. "I don't know when we'll return. They'll want to know."

She was right, of course. The standard rule was to be home by the time the streetlights came on. And if we couldn't be spotted on our street or within reasonable shouting distance, we had to forewarn about our whereabouts. It still holds true today, even though I'm entering high school in less than three weeks. But, again, that's another story. As I said, the library was a previously approved destination. So, I scribbled a hasty outline of our plans and secured it to the refrigerator with the cracked Chicago Cubs magnet.

"Here are our provisions." J. Dyanne was holding two brown paper bags. As we headed out, I peeked inside and was pleased to see my favorite cheese and crackers, plus PB&Js, apples and chips. It was going to be a long walk.

J. Dyanne collected our books; we slipped out the side door and walked the path to the front. Dog led the way, on the hunt for his favorite snack, old gum. It was still too early for much neighborhood traffic. The stone front porch where we normally convened with our friends was shady and inviting, but an excursion with J. Dyanne was hard to resist.

# Chapter 2 - In the Churchyard

We had gone no more than three blocks when the first signs of the extraordinary nature of the day pierced my consciousness.

Dog was sniffing an empty pickle bag, alternately licking it and sneezing at the sour taste. I loved those pickles, especially paired with salted pumpkin seeds. I remember thinking I'd get one at Frieda's Corner Stop on the way back. But the succeeding turn of events changed my plans.

We had just passed the Kirkwood place. Their camper was parked in the backyard. Its windows were open and the plaid curtains were blowing in the summer breeze. Crossing the alley and entering the short street of small shops, we were hit with the strong combined smell of hair and nail care products wafting from the Cut 'n Curl, which was oddly empty of customers.

We had crossed the busy intersection at Vincennes Ave. when J. Dyanne, a brisk walker, began to lag behind. We were near the new building of the neighborhood school. Always one to enjoy conversation, I was busy explaining my dreams of swords and sorcery, and so had not noticed what caught J. Dyanne's attention. At first I thought the book bag she carried was too heavy and was on the point of offering to carry it for a while. But cutting short my ramblings, I looked ahead.

The doors to the Methodist Church were open wide. Unusual, as it was a weekday. Further, a small news crew crowded a police car for space. And here were the neighborhood folks, murmuring and whispering amongst themselves.

A frisson went through the group as J. Dyanne and I came into view. The excited whispers got louder.

"There she is!" "She knew." "I bet she knew all along." I clearly heard Derek the delinquent, murmur, "Spooky, isn't it?"

Sixteen-year-old Patrice Kirkwood ran forward and clutched J. Dyanne's arm.

"Who did it? Where is he? Is he dead?" All this was panted out in a rush.

J. Dyanne shrugged out of Patrice's grasp as the small crowd held its collective breath. She studied the girl's tear-stained face. "So, it was Paul."

The whispers began again. "She knows." "She knew it was Paul!"

I too was startled. Patrice had not mentioned a name.

"Dyanne! You never said--"

She cut me off. "I'll explain later." J. Dyanne turned her attention to the nearly hysterical girl, who was again clutching at her arm.

"I can't think with you grabbing at me. Stop it!" Dog barked to emphasize the point.

Patrice closed her arms tightly across her chest. She was sixteen going on twenty-five. Face, figure and attitude were a natural for those *Jet* magazine models. Teenage acne wouldn't dare pop up on Patrice. Her hair was so wavy and long it looked like a wig, but she made sure everyone knew it was her own by flinging it around whenever possible. The boys seemed to like it. And although her smooth, tawny skin needed no makeup, she wore it anyway. She was used to getting what she wanted and made quite a racket when she didn't.

"You have to find him," she whined.

"I don't 'have' to do anything," J. Dyanne retorted. "He might just show up on his own. I don't know."

"Yes, you do! You know something or you wouldn't be here," Patrice insisted.

"That's completely illogical," J. Dyanne snapped. "Unless all these other people know something too."

If there's one thing that rubbed J. Dyanne the wrong way, it was ill-conceived deductions.

I intervened in my best journalistic manner.

"Patrice, can you articulate the scenario for us?"

She stared at me. I remembered that not everyone enjoys building their word power from the *Reader's Digest* like me, and yeah, I was showing off a little. As I mentioned earlier, I do love words. So I rephrased the question.

"What happened?"

Her puzzled look turned into a grateful and desperate plea. "Paul's been kidnapped. He could be dead! Or worse, crippled for life!"

I stole a glance at J. Dyanne, whose face showed not the slightest surprise. In fact, she didn't even seem to be listening, but looked restlessly around at the crowd. She let out a heavy sigh.

Patrice rambled on. It seems that just after 11:00pm the previous night, she received a call from Rev. Ingle demanding to speak with his son. Paul had missed his curfew and Rev. Ingle was convinced he was still with Patrice, his steady girlfriend for nearly two years.

Patrice swore Paul had left her house promptly at 10:00pm. By midnight, Mrs. Ingle was worried enough to have the Rev go and search Paul's known hangouts. Carl Porter from Frieda's Corner Stop confirmed that Paul had come in after ten. Patrice recited everything Paul had purchased like root beer, donuts, the works. By 1:00am the Rev returned home, but Paul had never reached the parsonage. A note was found taped to the front door from the kidnappers. That's when they called the police. At this point, Patrice ran out of steam.

Bewildered, I asked, "What did the note say?"

"They won't tell. They say it will compromise the investigation," the girl wailed. J. Dyanne was now staring at Patrice with a shrewd look in her eyes. The distraught teen returned the look.

"Well?" she demanded. J. Dyanne gave a short laugh and pushed on.

"Come along, Katrin," she said. "We've got a ways to go." I followed as best I could, Dog lapping at our heels. The crowd murmured at our backs, listening as Patrice continued her sob story.

"But, Dyanne, do you know something about this?" She kept walking.

"Perhaps. But I'm not going to discuss it in this crowd. You know I can't stand it." We pressed on, then, once clear of the crowd, she ducked back through the alley into the church parking lot.

We sat on a curb in the shade between Rev. Ingle's Buick LeSabre and a car I didn't recognize. J. Dyanne reached for the provisions, pulled out an apple and began munching. Her eyes were half-closed, not from savoring the red delicious, but from concentration. I recognized the signs. I went for the cheese, as with the hot weather, it would be ruined before long.

Biting into the crunchy saltine and soft cheese, I ventured a question. Sometimes these were welcomed, helping J. Dyanne's thinking process. I would know quickly enough if questions were an intrusion.

"How did you know this was about Paul?"

"It was obvious, Katrin. The commotion had to do with either the church itself or those connected to it. There was no apparent damage to the premises, so ergo, it was personal."

"But why not Reverend Ingle?" I queried.

"Would Patrice Kirkwood be hysterical over Reverend Ingle? Obviously, it wasn't the father, but the son." She continued munching. "Did you notice who else was there?"

I thought back to the scene. Nothing significant came to mind. "Just everyone you'd expect from the neighborhood."

"Coach Frazier?" countered J. Dyanne. "He lives over by the lake on South Shore Drive. What would bring him here, but news about his star running back? And did you notice Alderman Weaver's driver flirting with Joanie Stewart?"

At this point, I realized anew that even with my glasses, J. Dyanne saw much more than I. Now that she mentioned it, I did remember seeing the alderman's driver, Warren Murphy, looking as smooth as one of the tempting Temptations singers. He was smiling down at Joanie and must have been flirting, because Joanie's light-skinned face clearly showed the flush in her cheeks, which had nothing to do with cosmetics.

"Observation, Katrin. That's the biggest part of deduction."

"But admit it, Dyanne. You did know something more than simple observation."

She continued crunching on the apple. Again, she sighed.

"You're right. I did know something. It could have been a simple dream, but I should know better by now." She threw the apple core onto the grass and watched as Dog promptly disposed of it.

"This was the second one in as many days," J. Dyanne continued. "A young man, his face obscured, huddled in a darkened, cramped room. His right hand glowed slightly. Don't ask me why. His shirt had the number thirty-five on it and a crucifix was hanging on a chain around his neck. I thought it might be Paul, but you can never be too sure."

Okay, so I did know that J. Dyanne sometimes had dreams. The kind of dreams that often played out in real life. But it wasn't so much prophecy as an accumulation of information that seeped into the unconscious mind. Two months prior, I myself had an experience of this.

In early June, I dreamed I was preparing for a funeral and was undecided about a black hat. However, others in the dream told me not to make a decision because it hadn't been announced that the person had actually died. I woke to the radio newscast *pater familias* always blasted from the console in the living room on school days. The report was about the shooting of presidential hopeful Bobby Kennedy. My subconscious had been listening to the news; it wasn't a psychic dream. And neither was this, I was sure. I was also determined to maintain my focus on the case.

"But why kidnap a PK?" I insisted. "Preachers don't have a lot of money for ransom."

"Ah, but Paul is more than a preacher's kid, isn't he? He's being courted by any number of top-ranked colleges. He could be the next Gale Sayers. And yet, if his father's influence is as strong as some people think, high schools across this city won't have a football season come autumn."

I was stunned. This was, after all, a huge sports town.

"But there's always football," I protested.

"Katrin... you ought to read the papers more, and not just the comics."

It's true. It had been hard enough keeping up since April's tragedy of the Rev. Dr. Martin Luther King, Jr. and the ensuing nationwide riots. But since that June experience with news creeping into my dreams, I just went straight to the comics and sports. However, I'd somehow missed this tidbit of local sports news. It had probably been in the metro section, which was too close to the national politics of the day where it seemed like every time there was a leader to admire, somebody killed him. I just was not eager to read about worldwide riots or the next assassination with my morning cereal. My disquieting tangent into world affairs eased as J. Dyanne's steady voice brought me back to the present moment.

"Reverend Ingle advocates cutting sports programs. Too much violence between rival schools, both on and off the field. Too many drug-related incidents, again on and off field. He wants to bring the focus back to education and even religious studies, or at least prayer. And Alderman Weaver is listening. It could happen."

"I see. So you think somebody kidnapped Ingle's son as a threat or warning to ease up on his position?"

"Perhaps," mused J. Dyanne. "Even with high school sports, there's a lot riding on these games: money, careers, politics. So, perhaps--" J. Dyanne looked up, alert as a hunter. Listening intently, she rose and jogged over to the open windows facing the lot, keeping close to the wall. I followed. Voices carried clearly on the summer wind.

"You don't understand. I've got to!" Rev. Ingle's distinctive baritone boomed across the sill. A lower, calmer voice murmured a response we couldn't hear. But Ingle continued.

"They'll cripple him! You read the letter." His voice broke. "I'll have to recant. I'll agree."

Looking up through the trees and the dappled sunlight, J. Dyanne sighed. I knew that with this sigh, she'd solved it. Apparently, something in the voices on the wind clinched it, but it was still a mystery to me.

Leaving the windows, J. Dyanne led the way to the back door. It opened easily and we slipped inside. Dog was too pre-occupied with a squirrel to follow.

It was wonderfully cool inside the stone walls of the church. No need for AC down here. We traveled up the back stairs, past the nursery school and kitchens and up behind the sanctuary where Rev. Ingle had his office.

We caught the backs of Ingle, and two other men. The first was clearly Alderman Weaver, distinctive in one of his many Nehru jackets. Today's was a soft, camel colored linen. The second man looked like a plainclothes policeman. Who else would wear a corduroy jacket in this weather? They were heading toward the outer sanctum. Through the door we could see the church people steady praying.

"Call him," J. Dyanne urged. She was notoriously shy, but I wasn't about to call the Rev back from the sanctuary.

"Let's just follow and catch him on the way out." And so, trying not to look too out of place, we entered.

This was not unfamiliar territory to us. Many a Sunday morning found us here – J. Dyanne gracing the alto section, I in soprano. Not that we were particularly musical or religious. The choir director and church secretary merely insisted upon our presence. I suppose, since she was our mother, it gave her the opportunity to keep us under supervision while she was working.

Ingle and his entourage walked with purpose down the aisle, the Rev occasionally nodding to a fervently praying parishioner. He was a tall man who carried his weight well. I guessed he was somewhere in his late thirties. In any case, he was much younger than the old minister he replaced five years before and his relative youth and energy, coupled with chiseled features, had gone a long way toward re-vitalizing the congregation. Well, the female contingent, at any rate. His eldest son, Paul got his looks from his dad. Once Ingle was clear of the pews, J. Dyanne darted forward.

"Reverend Ingle," she called. He stopped in the vestibule and turned his signature, piercing gaze on us.

"Well, young lady, I'm in kind of a hurry right now," he intoned.

"Yes, I know. You're about to agree to the kidnapper's demands and you shouldn't."

"What do you know about that?" demanded the plainclothesman.

I didn't like his tone.

"With respect, sir, more than you," I asserted.

The uncomfortable silence was broken by the arrival of the choir director/church secretary, also known as "Mom."

"Katrin! Apologize." There was no sense in arguing. Though she wasn't very tall, *mater familias* (yes, Latin again. You guessed it... this means 'mother of the family.') was the kind of woman who easily took charge of a situation. She also had a very expressive face. Not much was hidden, even when she tried. Some looks were possible to negotiate. This wasn't one of them. It was the 'don't even think of disobeying me' look, so I did as I was told. However, J. Dyanne took up the case.

"There's more to this than meets the eye," she said, her attention turned to Mom.

The alderman was staring down at J. Dyanne. Alderman Weaver was about the same age as Ingle, but several inches shorter. And though Ingle was a solid family man, Weaver was notable for his fashionable style, his single status and appealing political charm. He turned that charm toward J. Dyanne. "Aren't you the girl who 'sees' things?"

J. Dyanne didn't seem to like his smiling face and stared right back, unblinking and unspeaking. This was just the sort of thing that was getting out of hand. Even the alderman believed the psychic rumors. J. Dyanne simply had the ability to connect the dots better than most, even if it sometimes happened in her sleep.

Mom intervened on J. Dyanne's behalf. "If she

says there's something more, I think you ought to listen. Remember Derek Fremont?"

Rev. Ingle considered a moment.

"Fine. But visions and dreams are all well and good in the Biblical sense, but I'll need more than that from you. This is my son. I need facts." He smiled grimly at J. Dyanne. "I'll listen to that, young lady."

I knew the 'young lady' reference wasn't going over well with J. Dyanne. His tone was what I'm sure the Women's Liberation women called 'chauvinistic.' But despite this, J. Dyanne decided to speak.

"The note – they said they'd cripple him if you didn't agree--"

"Hold on a minute. That information has not been published. How did you know?"

"Patrice."

"Kirkwood?" Ingle demanded.

"The girlfriend?" asked the plainclothesman.

"20 minutes ago," said J. Dyanne. "So you've gotta wonder, how did she get that little piece of info, right?"

"She must have seen the note," stated the plainclothesman.

"Of course she saw it. She probably wrote it," J. Dyanne retorted. "Unless she and Paul cut out little letters from the newspaper. If they had any sense, which I doubt, they should have used a typewriter or something."

"It was little letters..." Rev. Ingle began. "Wait, are you saying this girl... that my son... that this is some kind of stunt?!"

"She told you Paul left her house promptly at 10:00pm. Like anyone would believe that, unless she was trying to set up an alibi. We know the cashier at Frieda's Corner Stop saw him, cause he stopped by for three root beers, chips, a dill pickle, a twelve pack of donuts, a half gallon of milk and a pint of OJ. What does that sound like to you?"

"He was stocking up!" I exclaimed. It hadn't dawned on me earlier when Patrice was rambling on.

"Exactly. Yes, he's a growing boy, but he was supposed to be heading home. Surely you've got plenty of food there, don't you Reverend Ingle?"

"Of course. He's got a case of root beer in the basement. Swears it makes him fast." Rev. Ingle was growing more rigid with anger by the moment.

"Paul made sure someone saw him heading home. The mistake was, he should have had Patrice buy the food."

Once again, I was left amazed by J. Dyanne's swift grasp of seemingly innocuous details to piece together a puzzle.

"But where is he? He can't just disappear." The plainclothesman was getting a bit defensive. Alderman Weaver was looking speculative.

A dreamy look melted across J. Dyanne's face. I could tell she was tuning into something, the inner screen that put the puzzle pieces of images or random chatter into a decipherable picture. Then she smiled.

"Here's what you should do," she said. "And hurry. I think he might be hurt."

# Chapter 3 - Revelations

The crowd outside had grown. A second news crew was present and I recognized the familiar feline featured face of local journalist, Teri Brinker. She was the first black, on-air reporter at the city's local affiliate and often covered the stories on the South Side. Her cat-like green eyes were alert with curiosity as she directed the cameras in our direction as soon as she caught sight of Rev. Ingle.

He had just the right measure of righteousness in his manner as he strode forward, aiming straight for Teri Brinker.

"I've got a message. Turn that thing on," he demanded.

"We're rolling, Reverend," Teri asserted. "Go ahead."

Rev. Ingle faced the camera, his features schooled to a sternness only seen at the height of his most passionate sermons on sinners.

"I've made no secret of my belief that our young people are being co-opted by greed, by materialism, by worthless aspirations to fame and fortune, but neglecting the growth of their spirits which is the one thing that will sustain them through whatever life puts in front of them."

He paused the preacher's pause for impact. The crowd was hushed.

"I've got nothing against sports. I myself was a WLTA junior tennis player in my day. I admire our great athletes. Mr. Arthur Ashe, for example, is a personal favorite of mine. But I still believe that we can go too far in an all-consuming pursuit of competitive athletics. Drugs, fighting, gambling."

A tear coursed down his face. The man was good.

"And now, they've taken my son. The kidnappers want me to deny what I believe. They want me to withdraw my support of the resolution crafted by the honorable Alderman Weaver. They want me to oppose the proposition to suspend the coming high school sporting season – a proposition designed to re-focus our understanding on what matters in our children's lives – their education, their very souls!"

The crowd was with him now, shouting their support. Rev. Ingle was actually enjoying himself. All eyes were on him, except J. Dyanne's. I followed her gaze and saw Patrice, arms crossed and nervously gnawing her bottom lip. She wasn't shouting.

"Well, I've got a message for the kidnappers," Rev. Ingle continued. "They told me to say, in public 'I Agree.' That's all, just those two words. But people, I prayed on this. I consulted my heart, my Lord and the... best informed experts on this kind of thing..." He stole a glance at J. Dyanne.

“And I say this. I do NOT agree.”

There was a scream from the crowd. Patrice pushed her way through.

“How can you do that?! How can you doom your own son?”

Rev. Ingle turned to her. The cameraman got them both in the shot.

“You don’t know what you’re talking about, young lady,” Ingle said, in his most paternalistic voice.

“Yes, I do! Are you prepared to live with the... the guilt of sentencing Paul to a crippled life, unable to play the game he loves?” The tears that washed Patrice’s face were mixed with fear now.

“Who said anything about being crippled?” J. Dyanne said quietly. Patrice whipped around to face us.

“It was in the... everybody knows what the note...” Patrice opened, and then closed her mouth.

J. Dyanne was now on camera, but she didn’t notice. Teri Brinker was smiling like the Cheshire Cat – what a scoop for the evening broadcast.

“You told me they hadn’t released any information, yet you know the exact nature of the threat to Paul. Are you having visions now, as well?”

Without warning, Patrice lunged at J. Dyanne, but Dog was suddenly between them, barking protectively. Patrice wailed as she was grabbed by the plainclothesman.

“You’re a witch!” she cried. “A witch!”

Her screams were cut short when she saw a uniformed officer leading Paul Ingle forward, his left hand bandaged. Patrice broke free and ran to him.

"Paul! What happened? What happened?"

"Window in the camper," he muttered. "It slammed down on my hand. I think it's broken."

Coach Frazier hung his head in dismay. It looked like, regardless of Rev. Ingle's influence or not, the football season was already lost.

The reporters started to converge. The questions hurtled through the air. There was a familiar voice in my ear.

"Time for your fifteen minutes of fame, Katrin."

I turned away from the cameras, toward the whispered voice, but J. Dyanne was gone.

# Chapter 4 - True Talent

J. Dyanne and I lounged comfortably in the fading light of that summer's day. We were seated on the back porch now, trying to catch a late afternoon breeze. This was a refuge from the curiosity seekers out front and the constantly ringing phone. Requests were coming in to find lost dogs, missing property, racing tips, psychic predictions or communication with the dearly departed. J. Dyanne was seated on the glider studying the art of Johannes Vermeer, her sketchpad already full of fine pencil renditions of the great Dutch master. She had made the trek to the library after all, leaving me to tidy up the details for the press.

It seems Paul and Patrice had the bright idea to coerce Rev. Ingle to use his influence for the greater good. For them, the greater good meant saving Paul's senior year as Township High's leading candidate for future NFL stardom. Talk about dim.

There were still bits of it I couldn't piece together, like how J. Dyanne knew Paul was hiding in the

Kirkwood's camper.

"It was obvious, Katrin. You saw it yourself. The Kirkwoods came back from vacation two weeks ago. The camper's been closed up since. And yet, today, when it was nearly 90 degrees, the windows were open. Why? Because someone was in there. Again, why? They live in the new houses on the block, which have air conditioning. Why would they be in the camper... with the windows open?"

True, I had noticed the curtains blowing in the open windows. But it went completely out of my head once I'd heard about the alleged kidnapping.

"Patrice was telling the truth about Paul leaving promptly at ten," J. Dyanne continued. "But that's where it ended. He put in an appearance at Frieda's to establish the alibi, then doubled back and camped out in Patrice's family's trailer. But he couldn't turn on the AC; that would make too much noise and draw attention. Hence, the windows."

So simple and still I had missed it. I was beginning to mentally kick myself for my lack of perception, when J. Dyanne did that mind-reading thing.

"Don't feel so bad," she said. "You know I had help." Her head was bent over the sketchpad, almost as if avoiding direct eye contact.

"I certainly wasn't much help--" I began, but J. Dyanne interrupted.

"The dreams," she said. "You know, they're real."

"Well, of course they're real. Dreams are normal."

"Katrin..." she said, looking up at me. "They're true. My dreams are true. That's not normal."

It was a rare occasion when J. Dyanne actually looked worried. This was one of them. I tried my dream theory of facts being integrated through the sub-conscious, but she wasn't buying it.

"No, that's not it. I was hoping it was just a phase or something. But Aunt Alis says it's a talent."

"You talked to Aunt Alis? When? Where was I?"

"You were sleep. And... well, so was I."

Okay, so I admit, this was getting kinda strange. J. Dyanne having conversations with people in her dreams. And they were real.

"So, what else haven't you told me?" I said.

"Well, sometimes it happens when I'm not asleep, like that thing with Derek Fremont. I saw it all the minute he rolled out that stupid bike. But would he listen? No. Nobody ever listens."

"Reverend Ingle listened."

"Only because Mom convinced him," she insisted. She tossed aside her sketchpad in frustration and began pacing. "Katrin, I know this stuff and I really don't want to know it, so I try to ignore it, but if I don't say anything, I get nagged about it, actual nagging in my head, like it's some kind of obligation I have to fulfill. But then people don't want to hear it, or they get scared and start calling me names and it's just a waste of time mostly and I was hoping if I just stayed away from people it would go away, but it looks like that's not going to happen, so I'm stuck!"

She stopped pacing, snatched up her sketchpad and began to make furious strokes with her graphite pencil. I watched her for a moment, head down in case she couldn't hold back the frustrated tears I caught surging in her eyes. This was definitely a new side of Jacqueléne. I wanted to offer something that would help her feel better, but the truth is, what was unfolding was just a bit scary. So, naturally, I lied.

"I'm not scared." I picked up my Merlin book. "You can tell me anything." The only response was a sniff. "In fact, there's something you can help with." J. Dyanne looked up.

"Will the Cubs win the pennant this year?"

She then did what I hoped she'd do. J. Dyanne laughed – a good, long, loud laugh.

"No one can know that. Not even me," she replied, still chuckling. And suddenly, the muggy, heavy summer air felt lighter.

Jacqueléne Dyanne Dubois. She may not know everything, but as I learned in the months and years ahead, she knew a sight more than most.

## Chapter 5 - The Art of J. Dyanne

September 1968

Who knew 15 minutes could last so long? It had been over a week since J. Dyanne foiled the juvenile plot to influence the upcoming high school football season. As a result of her notorious aversion to media exposure and the ease with which she could slip away, unnoticed in a crowd, I had the *dubious* pleasure of seeing myself on the evening news and in the local papers for several days. Mom didn't make J. Dyanne go to church that Sunday because of all the unwanted attention. But Sunday afternoon Rev. Ingle and Alderman Weaver made a visit to 7541 to privately thank J. Dyanne for her assistance.

Since then, she retreated into solitary artistic pursuits that kept her from the public eye. But it's not easy to hide from your neighbors. She managed to sidestep the more ridiculous requests for her investigative assistance, except for Nicole Trotter. Who could resist the pleading eyes of a nine-year-old grieving for a lost dog named Buddy? You can't do it. She looked like a little coppery brown puppy herself.

Nicole had perched on the front porch for hours,

holding onto Buddy's collar, waiting for J. Dyanne to come outside. When she finally capitulated, Nicole explained how she and Buddy were running down the block, when Nicole tripped and fell. Buddy had slipped from his collar and continued racing down the block and around the corner. By the time Nicole got to the end of the block, Buddy was nowhere to be seen. Nicole's eyes were brimming with hopeful tears. J. Dyanne was holding Buddy's collar as she listened to Nicole's story. I saw J. Dyanne shiver a little, despite the warm afternoon. She was about to comment but stopped short as she looked around.

A crowd of kids had gathered by that time. This wasn't unusual, as our front porch, located in the middle of the block, was a natural meeting place of the neighborhood. It was where we met before setting off to play softball or go bowling. But this time it seemed everyone was expecting some kind of magic show. Naturally, J. Dyanne wasn't having it. She sent Nicole home and went back inside to finish her art project, still clutching Buddy's collar.

And so all eyes turned to me. I was peppered with questions about J. Dyanne. Was she really psychic? Did she really know everything? Who would be the next president? You name it, they asked it. By default, I, Katrin the Youngest, became the official spokesperson, although there wasn't much I could tell them.

But, unable to leave a puzzle unsolved or a lost puppy unfound, J. Dyanne followed up on Nicole's story later that day. She waited until it was nearly dark, the lull between outdoor daylight play and the cool breezes of nighttime porch sitting. The streetlights had come on, so we dutifully did our check-in at home and then prepared for our search. Naturally, J. Dyanne took provisions with her: a thermos of water, a package of Dog's Gaines-Burger, first aid kit, flashlight all packed in one of Dad's old canvas camera bags. She also brought Dog along, as it only made sense to utilize the assistance of a canine to find a canine. But I was sure she had sensed something else she didn't share. I was convinced when she pretty much went in a straight line to the vacant lot two blocks over.

I didn't much like this area after dark. There were stories that a local gang had buried a body in there. And though I'd never seen one, there was always the threat of rats and/or snakes. It was bad enough in the daytime, with sticker bugs catching on your socks, flies, and mosquitoes and everything else that made me miserable, but now in the near dark of a hazy summer evening, the unseen source of the rustling sounds was unnerving.

At the edge of the vacant lot J. Dyanne turned on the flashlight. She had Buddy's collar in her hand and let Dog sniff it, then followed him with the beam of light as he picked his way through the tall weeds, rocks and general debris. Fortunately, before my courage failed, they found Buddy with his hind legs stuck in the weeds in the middle of the lot. He was tired and dehydrated, unable to do more than whimper when we found him. J. Dyanne pulled away the weeds and scooped up the grateful puppy. Although I thought this was an excellent time to leave this desolate place, J. Dyanne took Buddy to a jumble of large concrete blocks and let him drink from the thermos cap. Since it looked like there was no rush to leave, I decided to get some answers.

"Okay, spill the beans," I said. "How did you know he was here?" J. Dyanne didn't answer right away. She was busy crumbling up the Gaines-Burger for Buddy and Dog. "It wasn't a dream. It was something else, right? Something about the collar." J. Dyanne finally looked up, while absently stroking Buddy's head.

"You're becoming very observant, Katrin. I take it you noticed my reaction when I first touched it?" I nodded. She took her time pouring more water for the dogs. She wasn't avoiding the issue. It was more like processing it, like when she would talk through one of her math problems.

"That was the first time it happened so clearly. Sometimes I can feel some kind of energy when I touch things. It's vague mostly. But this time, I saw a bunch of pictures in my mind. Interesting."

She rose. There was music coming from the porch of the closest residence and the laughter of a group of kids carried over from the corner. The dinner hour was over and the kids were back out. J. Dyanne tucked away the provisions, gathered up Buddy and handed me the flashlight.

"I'm not taking him back now for everybody to see." I understood her reluctance; she didn't need any more attention. We went home via a shortcut through the alley and installed Buddy on the back porch. Mom was okay with our plan to return him to Nicole's doorstep, anonymously, just after dawn the next day. We hoped this would defer suspicion. I almost ruined it by attaching Buddy's collar, but J. Dyanne reminded me that this would be a dead giveaway, since everyone saw her take the collar into the house. In the early dawn, we made the drop and got away without being seen. But we failed to consider the imaginative desire to believe in magic.

When the news of Buddy's seemingly miraculous return swept through the neighborhood, no one doubted that J. Dyanne had more or less conjured the puppy from thin air. Buddy's ecstatic joy when he next saw J. Dyanne didn't help. All doubters were now convinced, and Nicole Trotter became J. Dyanne's most adoring fan. It was a very good thing we'd soon be back in school. Kids wouldn't have time to follow us around ready to witness amazing psychic activity.

As the stifling dog days of summer began to flame out into fall, new stories took over and we were soon left in relative peace. The events during the final week of August gave people something else to talk about.

The big news, shown daily on television, was the rioting downtown. The whole world watched the police battle protesters, passersby and news media with tear gas, mace and clubs. Oh, and there was a political convention going on too.

The Female Teen Elder Other became infatuated with Georgia State Representative, Mr. Julian Bond and was inspired to go over to Grant Park and "get involved." And though the attractive Mr. Bond held a special place in her heart, the vibes at the Park were much too volatile and she left before any of the day's rioting started. She was thrilled when he was nominated to be the first black vice-president. But, alas, at 28 years old, he was too young.

Since all media eyes were focused downtown, J. Dyanne and I were left undisturbed while enjoying our last days of preparation for our annual scholastic endeavors. I would be entering my sixth year of study and J. Dyanne, her eighth. But there was one more hurdle to overcome.

The Labor Day weekend. This meant family gatherings, which could be very trying. The first of these was the raucous weekly Saturday night party, otherwise known as a bridge game, hosted by *pater* and *mater familias*.

Relatives from the maternal side of the family attended this bridge game. Aunts, uncles, grandparents, family friends... lots of hearty drinking, eating, signifying and, of course, card playing all taking place under the combined haze of cigar, cigarette and pipe smoke. They were the loudest games of bridge I have ever witnessed.

The good news for J. Dyanne and myself was that this week Aunt Gina, mom's eldest sister, brought cousins Marcus and Victor with her and they would spend the night. Also good was the non-appearance of the other cousins, courtesy of

Mom's younger brother, Uncle David – the eight-year-old terrible twins, Darla and Darlene.

On the surface, they looked like prim and proper Catholic-school girls, but underneath, well... let me just say, if anything went wrong, went missing, or was broken, you could safely say "the twins did it" with a 99% rate of accuracy. We usually saw them only on holidays like Christmas or Easter, so these Saturday night gatherings were twin-free and we could play gin rummy and pop popcorn without distractions. Then on Sunday morning we'd get to eat the leftover barbecue or fried shrimp and watch cartoons while everyone else slept late.

This Saturday the stirring events of the prior week were the topic of much loud talk in between heated analyses of bids made and hands played. Sporadic debates erupted about the chaos of the convention, the mass media coverage and whether or not all the protesting made any difference. A major tangent was a discussion about who actually elects the president. As usual at these times, I was sent to get the World Book Encyclopedia to prove or disprove someone's point. That night, it was to look up the entry on the Electoral College and read it aloud.

After the reading set off another round of debate, Aunt Velma, mom's next elder sister, pulled me aside and gave me a bourbon-scented hug.

"That's my little niece," she said. "Saw you on the TV. You should be one of them newscasters." Then, she pulled me closer, whispering in my ear.

"Where's your sister? She alright?"

"Yeah, she's fine. She's upstairs, painting. Why?"

"Just checking. She's about that age, you know." Actually, I didn't know what she meant. But she continued.

"You just... just take care, alright? You're the baby, but you gotta take care of her, alright? Alright?"

She seemed worried, so I assured her I would take care of J. Dyanne and she let me go, heading to the kitchen for another drink. I thought no more about her queries and joined J. Dyanne and the cousins to watch television.

This Sunday, there would be no cartoons. The overpowering heat of the previous week had been replaced with a cooling intermittent drizzle and gray clouds shaded the glaring sun. And, much to J. Dyanne's dismay, it was the day of the annual DuBois Family Reunion. She had been able to get through the influx of the maternal Watkins relatives on Saturday night by alternately watching television and painting, alone, upstairs.

Our room was still cluttered with the residual debris of a particularly complex foray into art. A notable artist in her own right, J. Dyanne humored the whims of the well-intentioned Great Aunt Alis – the aunt to whom she could, apparently, converse with in her dreams – by actually using the paint-by-number kits Alis occasionally sent to the premises at 7541. It was a kind thought, even though J. Dyanne completely disregarded the number scheme, painted well outside the lines, and generally exceeded the artistic level one would expect from such juvenile pursuits. In return, Alis had the completed pieces properly framed and placed proudly throughout her home.

The plan was to present the completed artwork to Great Aunt Alis that afternoon. This would be the highlight of an otherwise dismal day for J. Dyanne.

The annual Dubois family gathering took place in Washington Park the Sunday before Labor Day. Today. Our father had come from a large and continuously fruitful family. J. Dyanne was never completely at ease in their company, especially when gathered en masse. Hers was a consistently misunderstood personality. When pensive, enjoying the beauty of nature, she was thought to be aloof and unapproachable. And when able to clarify obscure points in adult conversations, she was considered to be, and I quote, a "smarty-pants." And as patience was not her strongest virtue, foolishness in others was not easily tolerated. Since society deemed her far too young to voice any such criticism of her elders, she mostly sat in stony silence while in their company. Not a recipe for good times.

However, Great Aunt Alis Graham-Andrews, whom the unkind amongst our cousins dubbed 'Gaa-Ga,' was an eccentric, and that made her interesting. Well into her 60s, Alis maintained a home in the city and a little cabin in the woods of Wisconsin where she spent her summers. And though her DuBois connection was through her sister's marriage to our Dad's father, she always returned to the city during the Labor Day weekend for the DuBois reunion. Aunt Alis did her own home maintenance, gardening, cooking and cleaning. She also liked to claim her preference of keeping her assets liquid – she disdained banks and kept her money hidden in secret stashes around the house. She took showers in the rain and told fabulous stories when she was in the mood. She was a fascinating Great Aunt, so J. Dyanne was usually eager to show her the result of her artistic endeavors.

As I entered our room though, J. Dyanne was staring balefully at the completed canvas. I was unsure of her unease; the painting was good. Perhaps it was the weather, which looked like it could easily end up in a downpour, thus canceling the event. However, considering her feelings about being with the DuBois folks, it didn't really explain the mood.

"Dyanne," I ventured. "Is something the matter?"

She merely looked at me. "The painting turned out really well," I prompted.

"It's not that," she replied. "Just feeling... a bit crowded today."

I didn't fully comprehend this response, but wanting to clear the heaviness in the room, replied, "Not to worry. Once in the park, you'll be able to stretch out."

"Not today." She looked out the window. The

drizzle was on pause at the moment. “No park today.”

Maybe she was thinking that with the recent rioting in the parks, it would be closed. But we had pretty much avoided that kind of thing on the South Side. Or, perhaps...

“Have you been having... dreams? With Aunt Alis?” J. Dyanne let out the tiniest of sighs.

“That’s just it... I haven’t. At least nothing coherent.”

Maybe the weather was affecting her signals or vibes or something. At any rate, I had come upstairs to choose my wardrobe for the day. The reunion was an event I actually enjoyed and always took great care in choosing the appropriate attire. But if there were to be no sojourn in the park because of rain, I’d need to re-think my ensemble.

“You think it’ll be cancelled cause of a rainout?” I asked.

“Not exactly.” She said nothing more, so I took this to mean that I should continue with my plans.

“You’re just uneasy about being around the DuBois clan all afternoon. The rain will stop and we can sneak off to the DuSable Museum with Marcus and Victor. That’ll soothe you.” A disinterested shrug was all the response I received.

I chose a Mom-made yellow and white vertically-striped cotton ensemble and began working on a suitable hairstyle. J. Dyanne, who disdained excess fuss about her appearance, had chosen jeans, T-shirt and one of her numerous hats. As we left to join the others downstairs, I remarked that she had left the painting, but she merely shook her head and continued out the door. Shrugging, I followed. Downstairs, Marcus and Victor were eating cereal while *mater familias* packed foodstuffs for the park.

"You might as well leave it all on the table," J. Dyanne murmured. "There's no rush."

She was told to hush and pack bottles of pop in the cooler.

"No one ever listens to me," she sighed. I felt she was developing a slight Cassandra complex. And I suppose she had reason, considering the number of times we let her remarks pass unheeded, even with plentiful evidence of her prescience. However, like the legendary Cassandra, the cursed seer of Greek mythology, J. Dyanne bore the burden and didn't complain. Much.

And then, the doorbell rang. The front doorbell. J. Dyanne and I exchanged looks. This couldn't be good, I thought. And so it proved.

# Chapter 6 - The Family DuBois

The last time the front doorbell had rung was when the firemen came to extinguish what they thought was a blazing fire in the basement. There was every reason to believe such was the case, as smoke was billowing out of the downstairs windows. It was left to me, the youngest, to explain to these fine city workers that certain uncles had convinced my father that they *could* roast a pig in the laundry room-turned-barbecue pit, in the middle of February. Just vent the smoke through the window.

What ran uppermost in my mind on the present occasion was that anyone familiar with the premises at 7541 came to the side door. Sometimes they knocked, but more often, they simply entered, unannounced. Ringing the bell meant it was a stranger. Or trouble. Today it was both.

The young man at the door claimed to be a cousin. I couldn't recall seeing him before. He was the advance guard, apparently. As I looked behind him, an entourage was coming up the front stairs. At its head, was one of the aunts. The formidable elder of aunts, Lucille DuBois Hamilton.

Upon her entrance into the foyer, she announced that due to the incipient inclement weather, The Family would gather here. She had already given everyone the address and they would be arriving shortly. All of them. Why Aunt Lucille had not invited everyone to her house she did not deign to explain. And sure enough, they came. In droves. Unfortunately, Great Aunt Alis Graham-Andrews was not among them.

Our immediate task was to clear away the remains of Saturday night's bridge party to make room for all the food and people. Barbecue grills were set up on the covered back porch, trays of potato salad, coleslaw, fried fish and chicken, spaghetti, cobblers, cakes and pies were available on every surface.

We, however, were careful to only eat food prepared by *mater familias.* Absolutely no one cooked better than our mom. Nobody.

Family crowded on both the front and back porches, the living room and kitchen, and definitely in the basement. Dad, who worked in construction, had converted the basement into a perfect entertainment center with the help of his brothers and nephews. A small space at the foot of the stairs had a poker table, next to which was a full bar with sink and fridge. This led to an open space that included a newly installed fireplace, in front of which set two recliners, a TV, a record player, and everybody's favorite: a regulation sized pool table. *Pater familias* had it installed, not only for his own entertainment, but also to keep the Male

Teen Elder from hanging out in pool halls. Better to have him and his friends in the basement instead of out in the streets getting in trouble. It worked for the most part.

Today, the competition was fierce. It was amazing how so many cousins thought they were pool sharks. They weren't. I'd been playing since I was eight and could easily beat most of them. But I didn't want to spend the day in the basement.

At the dining room table, Aunt Lucille was reviewing the DuBois/Graham Family History. She had anointed herself the family archivist. At each reunion, along with her apprentice and eldest offspring, cousin Shirley Hamilton Delroy, she updated the book with the year's newborns, reviewed old entries and added newly acquired details.

This project fascinated me. There were names, dates, interviews and stories. Aunt Lucille had taken the maternal side, the Grahams, back to the mid-1800's. She found African ancestors who had been sold into slavery and some who were freedmen, Native American relatives, and the odd European, mostly Irish, who showed up from time to time. And thanks to the DuBois Brothers Photography Co. – one of many creative though often short-lived "business enterprises" created by the uncles – there was an abundance of photographs from the '40s to the present to match the names.

It wasn't just a family tree. It was a journey into the annals of the DuBois/Graham lineage. It told of how best friends Alis Graham and Anne McDavid left Kentucky and migrated north to Chicago in the 1920s, followed by Maybelle Graham, the younger sister of Alis. The very fair-skinned Maybelle took after their father's side of the family, which was one of those occasional Irish-American ancestors in the family tree. Maybelle could have "passed" as a white person, but instead married the very dark-skinned John DuBois, who was a first generation Tennessean whose parents came from Haiti. The ten children from this union covered a spectrum of color from deep warm browns to soft creamy tans.

Anne McDavid, whose parents came from the racially diverse town of New Orleans, married Henry Watkins from Kentucky whose mother's people claimed native ancestry. The youngest children of Maybelle and Anne, *pater* and *mater familias*, respectively, turned the bond of friendship into one of family when they married.

The roots went deep with twists and turns, and seeing it all chronicled here made it solid. Aunt Lucille's pride in keeping the lineage documented was her testament to the survival of our family through difficult and tragic times. But I think the reason I was so fascinated was that, looking at this massive collection, I could see that though the stories weren't always pretty and romantic, joy also survived. I could sense the spirits of the ancestors backing me up and letting me know that I was part of a larger world than just the neighborhood and boundaries of Chicago.

To my surprise, Aunt Lucille actually noticed me, waving me over to an empty chair at the dining room table.

"Katrin, you were very well-spoken in that television interview. A credit to our people." I wasn't sure if "our people" meant our family or black people in general. Aunt Lucille was very concerned that we all were a credit to the black race, although she would never refer to us as "black," except when she was being critical. She really disapproved of the modern terminology that went with Black Power/Pride, etc. According to her, "proper folks" like us were Negro.

Aunt Lucille herself, like me, took after Grandma Maybelle. At birth I was pale white and gray-eyed with only my extremely curly, aka nappy, red hair to identify my parent's ancestry. Fortunately, I had browned nicely over time to my current caramel-like color and my eyes had darkened to match my father's hazel ones. I would have looked too weird otherwise. In fact, the story goes that when Mom brought me home, a squirmy thing four shades lighter than everyone else, my dear siblings told her to take me back because I looked so odd.

"Tell me, Katrin, where does your mother keep your photo albums?" She smiled, I think. It was hard to tell with her. Aunt Lucille was a notorious photo thief. I was saved from answering by the interruption of cousin Shirley.

"I must add details about your sister. How old is she now?" I was hesitant to give out too much information, but this was common knowledge, after all.

"Twelve. She'll be thirteen in October."

"Of course. According to my research, that's about when the talents emerge." Aunt Lucille didn't like this train of interrogation.

"That's enough, Shirley. Stop talking nonsense."

"Mother, you can't deny all the evidence. It's just like Grandma Maybelle, Great Aunt Alis and Ruth's mother. What's her name? Anne... Anne McDavid Watkins. They all had it."

"I said that's enough. I would appreciate if you would be silent." Everyone knew that tone from Aunt Lucille. I could see Shirley wanted to pursue her questions, but she refrained.

I was able to excuse myself and find J. Dyanne. Once the full component of family had arrived she, quite naturally, retreated to our room. But as none of our rooms were allowed to have locks on the doors, her solitude was soon invaded. By cousins. Dad had nine siblings, and they each had numerous offspring ranging in age from adults to babes in arm. And they had the run of our house.

After leaving the examination of the lineage to protect our privacy, I found J. Dyanne with Marcus and Victor examining her latest painting. When compared to the image on the cover of the kit, J. Dyanne had improvised an ivy-covered stairway that seemed to lead to a blank wall. She was in the middle of an artful analysis of her choices when an unexpected visitor came in... the young man who had rung the doorbell.

Not a bad-looking guy by any standard. His

smile seemed to fill the room. Although unfamiliar, he quickly made himself known. It was a complex connection. His claim was being a cousin by marriage through the maternal line to a niece of Great Aunt Alis Graham-Andrews; by name, James Spencer. Aunt Lucille acknowledged him anyway and had told him where he could find J. Dyanne. Apparently, he sought her out on behalf of Aunt Alis.

"Indeed," was all J. Dyanne had to say. I looked in surprise at her chilly reception. Here was a perfectly amicable and affable young man with a message from Alis and she was being more than indifferent, in fact, was being forbidding.

"Dyanne, I think we should hear him out."

"Indeed," she repeated. "Indeed we should." Marcus and Victor, sensing her distrust positioned themselves protectively by her side. The smile on Spencer's face dimmed a bit, but he proceeded.

"Aunt Alis sends you her regrets. She was really looking forward to seeing you. She speaks very highly of you."

"Don't sound so surprised," interpolated Marcus.

"Oh, I'm not surprised," he explained. "Just happy to meet you. I've read a bit about you, and followed the news reports with interest." He then turned his smile my way. My return smile came unbidden. He was nice. Those 15 minutes of fame had their perks.

Spencer continued. It seemed that Great Aunt Alis was planning to remain at her country cabin.

They were a little worried, because it was her custom to return to the city at summer's end. During his and the niece's last visit, they noticed that Alis seemed quite scattered in her mind. They thought it might be time for Great Aunt Alis to be under professional care.

"Why come to me? I can't do anything," J. Dyanne responded.

"Alis has always liked you. I was hoping you might come and visit, soothe her and convince her to come home where we can look after her."

J. Dyanne looked skeptical. Spencer pleaded his case.

"I've invited your parents to visit tomorrow. I hope you'll join them." His smile warmed up a few notches. "It would make Alis feel good." I could see the decision form on J. Dyanne's face even before she spoke.

"I'll go," she said briefly. Spencer looked relieved.

"Then I'll leave you to your little private party." He carefully closed the door behind him.

"You don't like him," Victor observed.

"No. There's something he's hiding behind that megawatt smile."

"Dyanne, don't be so suspicious. He seemed really sincere to me."

"Mark my words, Katrin. James Spencer has a plan. And I don't think I like it." She carefully placed the completed painting in her portfolio.

"Great Aunt Alis is in trouble."

We were headed into our next adventure.

# Chapter 7 - Alis in Wonder

The drive to Wisconsin was pleasant enough. As usual, J. Dyanne kept her thoughts to herself. This was one of those times when questions were definitely not welcomed. The driver attempted it once, and then let it be. He was just happy to be on the road. *Pater familias* was a traveler. We usually take a two-week road trip every summer. Last year we headed west to California and Disneyland. This year wasn't particularly conducive to road travel. With riots and rising tensions happening everywhere, we stayed close to home. So, hitting the road to Wisconsin in his beloved Buick deuce and a quarter was fine with him, conversation or not.

The navigator started singing show tunes; I confess. I joined in. *Mater familias* often entertained us at home on the piano when she learned some new sheet music. I often wondered if she had hoped to be a nightclub singer, but instead had the four of us and became a choir director. In any case, J. Dyanne effectively tuned us out in her own unique mental meditations on the moving landscape. The Teen Elder Others had remained in the city with their own pursuits.

When we arrived at Aunt Alis' bungalow, James Spencer was waiting on the porch along with who I could only assume was the niece. She did look vaguely familiar. A plain-featured woman, Janie Spencer compensated for her appearance with what I could tell was a flawless sense of style in the mod mode of the model Twiggy. She wore a geometric-patterned, sleeveless tent dress and strappy sandals, with her short hair straightened and slicked in a bob.

Alis was nowhere to be seen.

The Spencer megawatt smile was still there. The driver and navigator were welcomed with the offer of ice-cold beer. J. Dyanne, portfolio in hand, walked past them without acknowledgement. With a brief smile, I followed.

We found Great Aunt Alis seated on a lawn chair in the middle of the back yard. She was dressed in loose fitting jeans and an oversized gray sweat-shirt. A pair of sunglasses perched on her face and a flowered scarf was tied around her head. She wasn't doing much of anything. Just sitting there, which was very uncharacteristic. Alis was always doing something. Suddenly, she turned and faced us, pulled down the sunglasses and peered, eyes darting around. Then, settling on J. Dyanne, her face split into a quick, broad smile. Just as quickly, she returned her gaze to the horizon.

J. Dyanne breathed a sigh, seemingly of relief; her own face relaxed for the first time since James Spencer had approached us the day before. I was clueless what the exchange could possibly mean. It seemed to me that perhaps Alis was, indeed, going "gaa-ga." But J. Dyanne advanced with a light step.

"Hey, Auntie." She pulled up a seat on the grass at Alis' feet and propped up the painting. Alis slowly drew her gaze to it. She seemed pleased, and then grasped J. Dyanne's shoulder in a claw-like grip.

"You saw. I was hoping...." She picked up the painting and slowly traced her finger across the ivy-covered staircase. "It's close. You're learning."

"What? I don't know why I added that staircase."

"Have you talked to Anne?"

"Grand Anne? No. Why?"

"Well you've come this far, maybe it's time." Abruptly, Alis sat up. Then, in another swift move, she pushed the painting toward J. Dyanne. "Put it away. Quick." J. Dyanne carefully placed the painting back in its case as the Spencers approached with the parents.

"You girls having a nice visit?" Spencer asked. Janie had brought out lemonade.

"You'll be starting back at school next week. So, let's have a little celebration before we all head back to the city."

"I'm not going back," Alis said, to no one in particular.

"Sure, you are, Auntie. Don't you want to visit the girls on the weekends? You have such fun."

"It's my house, Janie. You'll get it when I die

and not before."

"And we all hope that's years and years away," Spencer swiftly interpolated. "How about some lemonade?"

"Jacqueléne. Katrin. I want to go for a walk." And without further conversation, Alis rose and briskly set off for the surrounding woods. I scrambled after her, J. Dyanne easily keeping pace. "Stay," Alis demanded, as Spencer took a step. Stunned, he stopped in his tracks, then laughed it off.

"Of course, Alis. You'll be fine with the girls."

We set off once again. Under cover of the trees, Alis peered back at the house. Convinced we were not being followed, she drew J. Dyanne close. "Listen girl, I've been sending you vibes for the past month."

"I wasn't sure it was you. It's getting worse. They kind of talk all at once. Especially when the family gets together. But I should have known it was you."

"Got that right. I'm not one of the dead yet. Took you long enough."

"You know I can't come without the driver."

"What is going on?" I asked plaintively.

"Katrin, I told you about the dreams. But there's also, like conversations, too."

"It's the ancestors," Alis explained. "They tend to be really talkative when they discover a likely mouthpiece." I still didn't understand. J. Dyanne sensed my confusion.

"When the family gets together the conversations start. More like requests. Tell the elder to stop eating so much pork. The boy needs to talk. Look out for stairs. There's no door."

It was becoming clear now. Apparently, the talent Cousin Shirley spoke about, that J. Dyanne was discovering, got confusing when the DuBois family came together. The spirits, though dead and gone, still couldn't stop trying to give advice and they cluttered J. Dyanne's mind with messages, which were sometimes hard to distinguish. No wonder those family reunions gave J. Dyanne such a headache.

"But what does Grand Anne have to do with this?" I demanded. "Are you communicating with her, too?"

"Not that I'm aware," she began.

Alis cut her off. "Listen, now is not the time. That niece of mine and her smooth husband know I put my money away in the house. But I can't remember where."

"Ah, the stair to nowhere. You're blocked," I concluded. J. Dyanne nodded.

"I couldn't figure out why I went there in the painting. It was you."

"Yes. I'm not as sharp as I used to be girly; and it's time you got some more practice."

"And now you expect me to find it before the Spencer snake."

"I'd be much obliged. I think they want to have me committed or something. That girl has to do something to pay for her clothes. She's just like her father; always trying to get the most with the least bit of work. That would be your so-called great uncle Clifton."

"When did they come here?"

"It's been about a month now. I was just finishing up a re-model in the master bath – you know, laying down some new tile, new sink and things. I usually have her come down for a couple of weeks. But she brought this new fellow. And she starts, real nice, talking about how at my age I need somebody to look after me. My age! And then that Spencer person always seemed to show up in rooms where he didn't need to be. Both of 'em. Sniffing around like dogs. Made me suspicious. So, I hid everything in a safe place."

"And... " J. Dyanne queried.

"I guess I should have used a bank, but you know, I like to keep my assets..."

"...liquid," I finished along with her.

"Auntie," J. Dyanne began, "I've never done something like this before."

"Sure you have. You just didn't realize you were doing it. Take a moment. How's the chatter?"

"It's quieter since we left Chicago."

"All you have to do is be still for a bit. Don't you try to think, just let it think for itself."

I looked on as J. Dyanne got a watchful, wistful look on her face. It was almost like she was waiting or listening as she stared through the trees. In a moment, it left and she was as alert and bright as ever. She turned to Alis.

"Do pennies in a can mean anything to you, Auntie?"

"There's a can next to the kitchen sink, but I know I've got more than that, girly."

"Well, it's a start. Come on, Katrin. Let the hunt begin!"

# Chapter 8 - The Psychic

We left Aunt Alis meditating in the wood and headed back to the house. J. Dyanne was moving at a fairly brisk trot, which is why I nearly knocked her over when she suddenly stopped. She stood near Alis' lawn chair in the middle of the yard and began turning in a full circle, like she was surveying the land. House, water pump, woodpile, well, an old outhouse, trees, metal link fence; a pretty wide-open space, with plenty of hiding places. I was relieved when she moved past the outhouse. Although unused, I had no desire to investigate in there with all its lingering smells.

"Where do we start?" I asked. "Do you think she hid something out here?"

"It's pretty obvious, but what we're really looking for is inside."

The only obvious thing to me was that I'd obviously missed something in my review of the yard. But there was no time to puzzle it out. J. Dyanne had already headed inside.

Mom was making bacon, lettuce and tomato sandwiches, while Janie fluttered uselessly around the kitchen. Knowing how fast J. Dyanne can move when she's on a trail, I quickly grabbed a sandwich. You just don't pass up Mom's BLTs. J. Dyanne headed to the counter by the stove, and reached for an old coffee can of pennies. James Spencer hovered around Dad, who was under the sink, working on the pipes.

"You know, Mr. DuBois --"

"Hand me the Stillson, will you?" Dad interrupted. Spencer had no idea what Dad was talking about, but J. Dyanne handed over the pipe wrench.

"Uh, like I was saying," Spencer continued. "I told Alis it's time to change all the plumbing."

J. Dyanne brought the can of pennies to the table and began rummaging through the contents. This caught Janie's attention.

"What are you doing? What's in there? That belongs to Auntie; did she tell you to look in there?"

Undeterred, J. Dyanne paid her no attention, but Mom doesn't like other people chastising her children.

"My daughter is not a thief." Janie started to mumble an apology when I noticed that J. Dyanne had become still, her hand inside the can.

"Did you --" I began, but she'd signaled my silence.

"She used copper pipes in the re-model and I told her, Alis, you need to re-do them all," Spencer was saying. "The property value of this place would double when it's time to sell this place."

That look was on J. Dyanne's face again. Something had clicked. She turned to Dad, who had finished working under the sink. Nothing was said, but Dad kind of nodded and began loading up the tools. He took a sandwich and headed out. And then Spencer turned his attention to the rest of us.

"Ah, Jacqueléne. Katrin. Did you have a good talk with Alis?" He got no response from J. Dyanne, who had pushed aside the can of pennies and was focused now on Mom's BLTs.

"You should try one of these sandwiches," I told him.

"I'm sure they're delicious. But I don't eat pork." He smiled at Mom, but it came off kind of flat. "Janie, honey, could you fix me a little plate of something?" Janie flounced to the fridge, while Spencer leaned back with a fresh can of beer.

"You have a very talented daughter, Mrs. DuBois. I've been admiring her artwork, especially the ones in the library. I have some questions for the artist." He leaned forward in the chair and put down his beer. "Will you show me?"

J. Dyanne was suspicious, but a nod from Mom and she rose.

"Come along, Katrin. You helped with some of those paintings, remember?" I hadn't, but I knew a signal when I heard one. Spencer didn't seem too pleased, but had to give in. His trademark smile was less warm.

Once inside the library, his good humor vanished altogether. In a serious tone that even I could see through, he began to speak of his concern for Alis and her mental health. How he and Janie wanted to help. Obviously, we could tell her mind was deteriorating.

"She seems like Alis to me," I answered. "She's just eccentric."

He had a different smile this time. I was beginning to wonder if he practiced all of them in the mirror so each one would perfectly match any situation. This one seemed to exude compassion.

"I can see you both love Alis," he replied. "But you must face facts."

"I still don't know why you're talking to us. We have no say in the matter," J. Dyanne responded.

"You have a gift. A talent. Isn't that what cousin Shirley called it? I think you can help." So, now we were getting to it.

"Alis needs care, and that care costs money. We know she keeps it here, but she claims to not understand what we're talking about." Now he arranged his face to one of anxious concern.

"Use your gift to help Alis, Jacqueléne. I believe, because you love her, you'll be able to 'see' what she's done with the money so we can give her the care she needs." He used a sad smile now. "Please. It will be the best thing."

J. Dyanne gave Spencer a smile of her own. One I'd never seen before. It was a bit scary actually.

"I'll try," she murmured. She crossed to the couch and sat, cross-legged, hands on knees and eyes closed. A low hum emitted from her throat. Her eyelids fluttered. It was quite a performance, and Spencer was buying it.

"Well? Well? What is it?" he demanded.

J. Dyanne came out of her fake trance and focused her gaze on him. Her voice was low and even lilted.

"Ah, you must have a bit of the sight yourself. You've guessed."

"What do you mean? I don't know anything."

"You just said it. 'Well.'" She gazed blandly at him.

It took him a moment, but Spencer was no dummy.

"She keeps the money in the well? That's ridiculous. I don't believe it. Try again."

J. Dyanne looked at him with displeasure. She dropped the low, lilting voice.

"You asked for my help. I gave it to you. That's all." She rose to go. Spencer now showed what must have been his most genuine smile, and it was mean. He didn't look remotely handsome.

"Not so fast, little girl," and grabbed her arm. Before I could attack, a voice of chilling severity echoed in the room.

"You will unhand my child." When *mater familias* used that voice, one was powerless to disobey. Spencer turned quickly, releasing his hold.

"My, uh, apologies, Mrs. DuBois. I'm so sorry," Spencer spluttered. "It's just... we're so worried, and the girl--"

"The girl and the rest of us are leaving."

J. Dyanne rushed forward.

"We've got to stay. I need to talk to Dad." And she ran out the door. I followed, although I really wanted to witness the scene I was sure Mom had in store for Spencer. But first things first.

We found Dad in the basement. There had been

a leak resulting from the handiwork Alis had done in the bathroom. He was applying duct tape to secure a shiny copper pipe. J. Dyanne watched him with shrewd eyes.

"You found it already," she said.

"What took you so long?" Dad queried. I looked between the two of them, completely confused. Alis came briskly downstairs. One look at the pipe and she clapped her hands.

"I knew I put it in a safe place," she said. "Well, girly, your message was a bit mixed up, but you'll get better."

J. Dyanne saw my total lack of understanding and once again explained.

"Liquid assets, you see? Hide in plain sight." She pointed to the copper pipe near Dad. "In the wood, I pictured pennies in what I thought was a can. But when Spencer mentioned copper pipes, it clicked." Alis smiled at J. Dyanne like a proud teacher looks at her prize student.

"Your talent gave you an image of copper, the pennies, and a cylinder, which you saw as something familiar to you, an old can." She gave J. Dyanne a hug. "I guess you don't do much plumbing."

"But, your money is in the pipe? How is that safe?" I asked. Dad laughed. Apparently everyone knew the answer but me. Taking pity on me, he started pointing out all the pipes.

"This is the main water line. And you've got your hot and cold. So what is this other pipe?" he said, pointing to the shiny copper bit. "Think about it."

Looking more closely I could see that the end of the copper pipe was attached to an exterior wall. Looking out the window, I could see that it didn't go through – it ended at the interior wall.

"Oh! It's a... like a dummy pipe. It looks like it goes somewhere, but it goes nowhere." And then something else dawned on me. "Like the stairway to nowhere in the painting!"

"Very good, Katrin," said Aunt Alis. "Jacqueléne knew, even when she didn't know she knew. You both just need a little more practice."

I knew then that life was going to get a lot more complicated.

# Chapter 9 - Cassandra Lives

Although I missed out on seeing Mom's confrontation with Spencer, I did witness Dad escorting him and Janie off the premises. Technically, they had done nothing illegal, which Janie continually shrieked, but only because they never got the chance. Maybe not illegal, but it was still wrong. Dad made that very clear. They were also informed that they would have to answer to him if they ever showed up again.

After their departure, we sat down and polished off all the BLTs and lemonade. I couldn't help but regale them with the tale of J. Dyanne's psychic performance in the library. The memory of the fake trance revelation about the well still had me in stitches. Alis winked at J. Dyanne. I looked between the two of them.

"What?" I asked.

"Alis does have a stash in the well," J. Dyanne explained. "All part of her 'liquid assets.' But, there you go. Spencer didn't believe me."

"Don't you worry about that. Sometimes it's better if your enemy underestimates you."

"But I don't have any enemies." There was an

extremely quiet pause in the room. "Do I?" J. Dyanne added. No one spoke.

"Well," I piped up, "I'd say Patrice Kirkwood isn't a big fan."

Mom got up from the table and started to clean. Dad leaned forward.

"Jacqueléne, I wouldn't say you, personally, have enemies. But you need to understand, there are people who just don't like the talents you have." Then it hit me. The look she exchanged with Dad in the kitchen. He knew. He had them, too. I couldn't remain silent.

"Wait. Hold on. Does everybody around here have talents?" I asked. Alis looked a question at *mater familias.* She looked to *pater familias.* He polished off his beer. Alis broke the silence.

"Ruthie, I think it's about time."

"Mama should do it," she muttered.

"But Anne's not here now is she?" Alis countered. This was making me very impatient.

"Mom, what is it Grand Anne should do?" I asked. She turned away and leaned heavily on the sink, saying nothing.

"Anne can give them the details later, Ruth," Alis persisted.

"Fine. Go on," Mom said. "But you call and tell her what you've done, not me."

"Don't you worry about Anne. I'll handle that." Alis shifted in her chair and turned to me and J. Dyanne.

"Katrin, everyone, to some degree, has what you might call intuition. Most people ignore it or chalk it up to coincidence or just a feeling. You know, like a gut reaction or something. And for some, it's more heightened and they accept the occasional incident of extra awareness as part of their lives."

She paused, again looked at Mom, who was now vigorously washing dishes, her back to the room.

"And then there are those who, unmistakably, have a powerful talent," Alis continued, "able to access the sensory energy of the world around them. They can even learn to work with it, harness it, utilize it to make change. Your sister is showing clear signs that she has these talents." Alis turned to J. Dyanne. "What are you now twelve, thirteen?"

"I'll be thirteen next month."

"There you go. It's been showing up for a while now. But we couldn't tell if it was going to stick or not."

"We? Who else knows about this? Why didn't anyone tell us?" I demanded.

"It's on a need-to-know basis, Katrin. If you exhibit the signs, it gets explained. There's no reason to broadcast it to just anybody. Besides, sometimes kids grow away from it, can't or won't work with it, and it gets suppressed."

"And sometimes it gets suppressed by others," Mom said from the sink. Alis didn't immediately respond, so Dad picked up the thread.

"We're talking to both of you because there's something you should know," he began. "The kind of talent Alis is talking about scares a lot of people. They don't understand it, so they fear it. And when people get scared, they can be dangerous. I want you to look out for each other."

I remembered how that Spencer character got angry with J. Dyanne. I was ready to jump in and protect her and was glad Mom came in. I began to understand why she was always so protective of us. It wasn't so much as being too strict. She just wanted to be sure we came to no harm from outsiders who were frightened about whatever it was that made us different.

I was about to ask Mom if her talents had been suppressed when she suddenly became very brisk and businesslike.

"Okay, we'd better get packing if we're going to make it to Chicago before morning. Alis, why don't you and the girls collect all your 'liquid assets?' I'll start on your suitcase. Raymond, you can make sure Alis' car is ready to go." And with our marching orders, we set about bringing Alis home.

The drive to Chicago was pretty quiet. No show tunes this time. The navigator had the look of silence on her face and chain-smoked Winston cigarettes. Fortunately, it was one of those easy, end-of-summer nights when the wind whispered through the windows as the car sped on the open road. It had been an eventful and informative day. I could sense we were heading down an entirely new path now and it might not be all smooth going.

Well, I may not be as talented as J. Dyanne, but I knew when to keep my mouth shut and go with the flow.

# Chapter 10 - Grand Anne

There was still a day of rest before school started. Since we missed the previous day's Cubs double-header because of the Wisconsin adventure, our plan was to split the day between organizing our school supplies and watching today's game. But Mom had a different agenda. Without much explanation, she bundled us into the car. I couldn't tell right away where we were headed. It was in the opposite direction from the grocery store. She drove past the church and continued along what is usually the bus route to school. But then she turned down an unfamiliar street and pulled up in front of a vaguely familiar storefront, called 'Yemaya Candle Shop.' And then it clicked. We were coming to visit Grand Anne.

Both of our maternal grandparents had an acute aversion to being called such things as Grandpa or Granny. Neither of them felt these titles matched their rather active and unusual lifestyles. However, they did require the respect due to their years. Both did feel they were indeed grand, so we have, since my earliest years called them Grand Henry and Grand Anne. Separated, though not quite divorced, before I was born, Grand Henry and Grand Anne were cordial with each other and attended most family functions. These events also included Grand Henry's good friend Joan, who figured as an aunt-like addition to the family. We called her... Joan.

But I digress.

I'd heard a few stories about Grand Anne's candle shop. But it was a rare occasion when we actually visited the premises. I hadn't been here since I was about four or five years old.

You see, Yemaya wasn't just a candle store. It was a treasure house of mystery, or so it seemed to me. Candles were the least of it. There were fragrant oils for any and all ills and health. Herbs, powders, incense and amulets. Paintings, books, singing bowls and chimes. I was eager to get inside. J. Dyanne was less so.

The store looked closed, but Mom was determined. She marched us around to the side door, which stood slightly ajar. Without hesitation, she pushed it open. We entered the back room of the store and found Grand Anne just taking a steaming kettle off a hotplate.

No ordinary shopkeeper, Grand Anne was more like an elegant hostess. She wore her wavy hair braided and wrapped around her head. And though her dresses harkened back to the 1940's, they never looked worn out or dowdy. Just, well elegant.

The small table was set with porcelain rose patterned teacups and chocolate chip cookies on matching plates. Bundles of dried herbs and plants hung from hooks along one wall. Jars of spices and boxes of scented candles lined another. A television was situated on a tall stool in the corner, next to a desk. I took a deep breath... apple spice tea. Grand Anne's special blend. She had obviously been expecting us.

"Good to see you, daughter," she said by way of greeting. Mom simply nodded and closed the door. Nothing else was said and something in the air kept me silent. I stood looking from Mom, to Grand Anne, to J. Dyanne. I'd never seen *mater familias* so tense before. Grand Anne poured tea. We sat around the table. I tried to catch J. Dyanne's eye, but she was looking down at her cup. I felt like there were conversations going on that I couldn't hear. My suspicions were confirmed when Grand Anne spoke.

"Now, you know that's not true Ruth. I'm more aware of the situation than you can possibly imagine."

"Yes, mama, we all know I don't have your talents."

"That's not what I meant, but since you mention it, remember... it was your choice, daughter. Your choice."

"And I don't regret it. Although you can't possibly imagine that."

The clattering of J. Dyanne's cup as she dropped it onto her saucer seemed to break the tension of the room. Grand Anne looked from J. Dyanne to me and sighed.

"You know this is irregular," she said. "Neither

of them is of age."

"And you know that's not set in stone," Mom replied. "You and Alis were even younger when your caretaker began working with you. Besides, you saw the newspapers. People are starting to take notice."

It was becoming hard for me to keep track of what Mom and Grand Anne were talking about. I started to speak up, but J. Dyanne signaled me to wait.

"They start school tomorrow," Mom went on. "They know very little about what to expect or how to prepare. You're the caretaker. It's time."

Caretaker? Was Mom turning us over to Grand Anne? Before I could get too anxious, Grand Anne took my hand.

"It's okay, Katrin." She sighed again. "Fine."

Grand Anne rose and crossed to the desk. It was an old-fashioned roll top model with several drawers on each side and each drawer had a keyhole. I wondered what she kept in there that needed to be locked up so tight. She pulled a silver chain from around her neck. A locket and several small keys dangled on the end. She fitted one of the keys into the center desk drawer and removed a carved wooden box and brought it to the table.

"Come on and pull your chairs closer." J. Dyanne and I scooted around. Mom stayed where she was.

In the center of the box lid was a smooth, copper rectangle etched with four symbols: a spiral, a circle resembling a coin, a bowl of fire and what looked like the dome of a temple.

"This," said Grand Anne, "is the Traveler's Box." She opened it and removed a royal blue, velvet pouch. She set the box aside and removed an ancient-looking book and an elaborately illustrated deck of cards tied with a golden ribbon. These weren't regular playing cards. For one thing, they were slightly larger. I'd seen tarot cards before, but the image on the cover didn't look like those I had seen.

"You're right, Katrin," said Grand Anne. "This is not tarot deck. Some like to call them oracle cards, but I simply think of them as cards that carry wisdom." I began to gingerly look through the book, while J. Dyanne examined what looked like hand-painted artwork on the cards.

"As you two have noticed, you're traveling a new road. There have been generations before you and there will sure to be those to follow. These cards, this book, are tools to guide, to support and hopefully lead you to your goal."

"What goal?" J. Dyanne asked.

"I wouldn't know. That's for you... each of you, to find out."

The cover of the book was illustrated with the figure of a smiling boy holding a flaming torch. He looked scruffy and smudged with dirt; his clothes were tattered and probably belonged to the fashion of at least a century past.

"Who's this?" I asked.

"That," said Grand Anne, "is The Linkboy." And then she closed her eyes and began to talk. I loved listening to Grand Anne talk. She grew up in Kentucky and her voice still carried a soft southern caress.

"Imagine if you will, a world without electric lights. And think about what it would be like trying to walk the streets on a moonless night. There were no bright streetlights as you know them today, only scattered gas lamps and in some places no lamps at all. Poor street urchins would find some meager profit by making a torch, called a link, and offer to lead people to their destination. They were known as linkboys. In the same way, The Linkboy in these cards lights your way."

"Why is his face in shadow?" asked J. Dyanne.

"You've picked up on a key issue, Jacqueléne. Linkboys were very useful. They did, indeed light the way. However, the awareness a traveler needed to maintain was whether the Linkboy's light led to the traveler's goal or down a dark alley that ended in betrayal."

"How are you supposed to tell the difference?" I expostulated.

Grand Anne placed the book and cards back in their pouch, and carefully tucked them into the box.

"That's up to the traveler to learn. Work with these and you'll not fail."

Mom started to protest, but Grand Anne held up her hand.

"That's all for now, daughter. Not to worry." I could tell that's not what *mater familias* wanted to hear, but she held her counsel, and that was really unusual. There was plenty to think about, so I didn't dwell on it. I could hardly wait to get home and study the cards. All thoughts of the Cubs game went out of my mind.

Once home I found J. Dyanne less than enthusiastic about the Traveler's Box. She was more interested in completing the organization of school supplies and taking score of the televised ball game.

We already had our brand new bus cards. My book bag was soon packed with a new notebook, pencil case and blue Bic pens and I already decided what I would bring for lunch, though not in a lunch box this year. Too juvenile. A brown paper bag would do. And I had already laid out my new school clothes.

Sometimes, because of financial necessity, Mom made clothes for us. I really liked what she created, unlike J. Dyanne. This year, however, I had a store-bought, long-sleeved, red dress, decorated with brass buttons at the cuffs with more at the collar and down the front. White knee socks and black patent leather shoes completed the look.

With all school prep complete, I cleared off the dining room table and set out the Traveler's Box. J. Dyanne turned on the television. She gave every appearance of being enthralled with the game, but I saw her glance my way several times. I didn't push. Besides, the cards were fascinating and required my full attention.

There were sixty-five cards in all, with three divisions. The first was the main set of forty-four

Wisdom Cards with four designated goals: Duty, Well-Being, Abundance and Affinity, which were like the suits in a deck of playing cards. Duty was represented by a red flame, Well-Being by a green spiral, Abundance by a yellow coin, and Affinity by what looked like a rising sun, except it was blue. Each goal had four trump cards: Traveler, Relative, Caretaker and Warrior and an additional seven levels. Then there were twenty cards that represented the elements needed by a traveler, like Courage, Respect, Discipline, or Love. And then there was one Linkboy card. Once sorted, I saw that the images also represented the spectrum of world cultures, referencing each continent on the planet. The book gave detailed instructions and explanations for each card and it wasn't long before I did my first Wisdom Reading.

At the bottom of the box was a silk cloth with the reading layout drawn in gold. It was shaped like a dome with specific placement for a card reading. At first it was a little tedious looking up the meanings for each card, then trying to link all the themes, but in the end the results seemed to indicate that I was either going to become a warrior goddess fighting to save the world or be the first female shortstop in major league baseball.

Next time, I would study the cards without the game on.

## Chapter 11 - Back to School

The school year began in the usual way. For me, that meant excitement. Since first grade, after adjusting to the initial shock of kindergarten, I looked forward to the first day of school. It was like New Year's Day for me; the beginning of a new quest into unknown territory, though set in the familiar structure of the classroom. And, call me crazy, but I loved the smell of the school on the first day. The wooden floors newly lacquered, the bulletin boards still waiting for new student artwork and essays, new lessons, new ideas. Before deciding to become a doctor, I used to think about being a teacher, just so I could stay in school forever.

For J. Dyanne, it was different. It's not that she didn't like school. She did. And she excelled in her studies. It was just that there were people there, and you know how she gets in crowds.

I suppose I should mention that the predominant school population at Nightingale Elementary was white. When I arrived in the third grade, there were only six black students at the school. *Mater familias* had taken advantage of new desegregation laws and the permissive transfer system and sent us from the neighborhood school to the southwest side to "broaden our horizons," as she called it. It took some getting used to being surrounded by the kind of people I'd normally only see on television.

We took public transportation at the corner of 75th Street all the way to the western end of the line and then a five-block walk to the school. Although we did experience some incidents of resistance, it was a fairly smooth transition. It turned out that being the smart kids actually worked to our advantage. At least nobody could call us stupid.

Returning to Nightingale, it would be good to see the school friends who were different from my neighborhood friends. At school I had friends with names I'd only read about in books, like Meg or Betsy, who also loved horses. Of course, I should talk. I was named after a Norwegian character from an old book Mom had read.

At Nightingale there were kids here whose parents had emigrated from places like Greece and Lithuania. They also introduced me to TV shows I'd never watched before like *Kiddie A Go-Go.* Everybody talked about it at school, so I'd rush home to see it. Nobody else in my neighborhood did. Clearly, the kids on this show, who all looked like the majority of kids at school, danced... well let's say it was different from what I was used to. This year the television spectrum had expanded. There was a new show, *Julia.* Now, I could tell my school friends to watch a show about people who looked like me. And even though recess only offered the skill of jumping with a single rope, since double-dutch was not yet available in this part of town, I was glad to be back at school.

This year, there were more transfers. One of them was in my class, Russell Phillips. He was nice enough for a boy. The annoying thing however, was that everyone started to insinuate that he was my boyfriend, just because we were from the same minority group. Sure he was kind of attractive, in a rugged sort of way, but the matchmaking assumptions and teasing were enough to leave me feeling very contrary. Even the teachers started pairing us up on school projects. Gee, how cute was that? But this was a minor annoyance.

The first indication that this was not going to be the usual scholastic year came when I was called out of Home Economics by the vice principal. The message came just as I was getting the hang of darning socks. Yes, we were actually spending school time learning the archaic practice of darning socks. Go figure.

The office of the vice principal, Mrs. Dwyer, was a slightly oversized closet with just enough room for her desk and two visitor chairs. The walls were lined with five-drawer, metal filing cabinets. It was rumored that Mrs. Dwyer maintained a file on each student from birth to death – the J. Edgar Hoover of Nightingale Elementary. I wasn't sure she could be trusted, even though her smile was friendly enough. Can't say that I cared for her style of eyeglasses – powdery blue with rhinestones twinkling on the frames. Her eyes were the same powdery blue, so the glasses kind of blended into her pale, powdery face. Except for the rhinestones. But that's beside the point.

The point was she had J. Dyanne's file open on her desk. In it was a clipping from our neighborhood paper about the August incident with Patrice. It was the article that carried the infamous "South Side Seer" headline.

"Katrin Elizabeth Dubois," she crooned. "What a pretty name. Please, have a seat." I took a step toward the chair. "Close the door, thank you." That sealed it. If the room seemed small with the door open, closing it reinforced the cramped, closet-like feeling. I'd read once about claustrophobia. That would explain why I felt anxious. That, and J. Dyanne's open file.

"I'm sure you must be surprised I asked to see you. Nothing to worry about. Let me assure you that neither you nor your sister are in any trouble." My eyes must have moved toward the newspaper clipping.

"Oh, you're wondering about this? Well, I think it's important for me to know as much as I can about all of the students here. That way I'm able to support each of you." She seemed sincere, but the feeling of suspicion swam around the room like a chill whisper. Despite the closeness of the space, I felt cold.

"So, tell me Kat, how are you doing? How is Jackie?"

"We're fine."

Mrs. Dwyer continued to peer through her glasses. I guess she was expecting more. I didn't say more.

"I've noticed that Jackie--"

"Jacqueléne," I interrupted. "She really prefers Jacqueléne." This wasn't exactly true, but Mrs. Dwyer didn't know either of us well enough to give us nicknames. I didn't say this out loud, mind you, but Mrs. Dwyer took the hint and made a note in her file.

"Very well, Katrin. Your sister seems to be less social this year. She often sits alone at recess. I hope this media exposure hasn't caused her to become a loner."

"Actually, she uses recess to study more. She graduates this year and wants to get into Lindblom Tech. She has to take a test, you know."

Mrs. Dwyer took more notes then looked at me, her eyes glinting.

"Then I'm sure she doesn't want these rumors about odd behavior to spread around." Again, she looked expectant for a response. I simply looked back at the glasses.

"Well, that's enough for now. I'll keep this information private. We'll want to ensure a quiet learning environment here at Nightingale."

I had risen from my chair when she spoke again.

"There's no need to worry your sister about this little talk we've had. I wouldn't want her to be distracted in any way while she studies for her tests."

I didn't quite understand her meaning. Of course, what she didn't realize was that, even if I wanted to, which I didn't, I can't really keep secrets from J. Dyanne. In fact, during lunch I spilled the beans. She took the news that Dwyer was spying on her quite calmly.

"I figured," she mumbled, talking through her turkey sandwich.

"Maybe you should mingle more."

"No. I can't. You don't know... all these people. You'd be surprised at how much energy it takes to block out all their thoughts and emotions. It's much worse this year." She glanced around the lunchroom. "Linda is worried her parents will get divorced. Patrick has a crush on Susan; she has a crush on Michael. It goes on and on. I can only shut them out in class or when I'm drawing." Her glance fell on the science teacher. "And there's something about Mr. Gordon."

"What?"

"I don't know what. It's just... something."

J. Dyanne's talents were coming along strong. I hadn't realized things had progressed this far and remembered Aunt Velma telling me to look after my sister. Now I could see why.

September was going along fine, until the incident where J. Dyanne got the math teacher fired. It wasn't on purpose. She really liked Mrs. Martin, who loved mathematics as much as J. Dyanne.

See, what had happened was, a bunch of students during lunch were complaining about the last math test and their general lack of appreciation for Mrs. Martin's teaching skills. I have to say, math isn't my all-time favorite subject, but I actually liked this teacher. Unable to stand the whining, J. Dyanne said, loud enough that the entire lunchroom heard, that they'd better be glad we had Mrs. Martin because next semester she was leaving to have a baby and the new teacher probably won't be as nice.

The problem with this was that Mrs. Martin had told no one about her impending motherhood. Her plan was to keep her pregnancy a secret until the end of the school year so she would not have to take the compulsory unpaid maternity leave. J. Dyanne's spontaneous foretelling of her delicate condition forced the issue.

The good news was that in the spirit of the rising feminist movement, Mrs. Martin filed suit against the school board, as it was really ridiculous to think that a woman couldn't teach if she was pregnant

Naturally, this incident had some expected repercussions. People started whispering and pointing. It didn't help that George McIntyre, a transfer from our neighborhood started spreading stories about J. Dyanne in school. What had been a fairly local phenomenon of rumors began penetrating the classroom.

Mrs. Dwyer, however, did a surprisingly good job of easing suspicion by convincing the faculty that J. Dyanne had advanced powers of observation. For instance, she had probably noticed that the newly married Mrs. Martin was often tired, and subject to dizzy spells. She even suggested to Mr. Gordon, who taught science, to utilize J. Dyanne in a presentation on the necessity of keen observation in the application of the scientific method. This tactic actually led most people to remember that J. Dyanne had always been a brainiac rather than a weirdo. I suppose Mrs. Dwyer was sincere about wanting to *"ensure a quiet learning environment here at Nightingale."*

Mrs. Dwyer had another surprise up her sleeve. The eighth grade Social Studies class was covering municipal government. She had gone to the trouble to contact our neighborhood representative, Alderman Weaver to suggest he mentor J. Dyanne, allowing her to intern in his local office and perhaps visit the City Council chambers. This would qualify as extra credit for her. Surprisingly, Weaver had agreed. He came smiling up to Mom at church that next Sunday, along with Rev. Ingle.

"Mrs. Dubois," he said, doing the politician's handshake and smile. "I am very pleased to have your daughter as a Jr. Alderman. I'm sure she'll be a great asset to my team."

Mom looked a bit skeptical, and I don't think it was about J. Dyanne's abilities.

"Actually, you'll have two of my daughters at your office. Katrin has been assigned as a reporter for the school's paper."

Weaver looked over at me. His smile didn't waver, but his eyes held a speculative look that I'd seen before.

"You'd better be on your best behavior, Alderman," chuckled Rev. Ingle. "These are two sharp young ladies." He winked at us and moved on to greet his other parishioners.

That afternoon we consulted the Wisdom Cards again. There were no baseball distractions this time. The Cubs had ended the season with a winning streak, though they finished in third position. Maybe next year they'd win the pennant.

J. Dyanne had finally come around to studying the cards. In her usual methodical way, she first read the book, and then examined each card, its symbols and meaning. She preferred the aspect of the cards that allowed the reader to gain insights, rather than the fortune-telling element. She had plenty of that to deal with on her own. This type of Wisdom reading only required seven cards instead of the usual thirteen.

The first two cards drawn were placed at the Traveler level on either side of the base of the dome spread. This represented the positive and negative aspects of the question. The next four cards were placed in order from bottom to top of the dome's pillar, which corresponded to the four goals: Duty, Well-Being, Abundance and Affinity. The seventh and final card was placed sideways across the top of the dome. This was the Teacher position, the cumulative final insight.

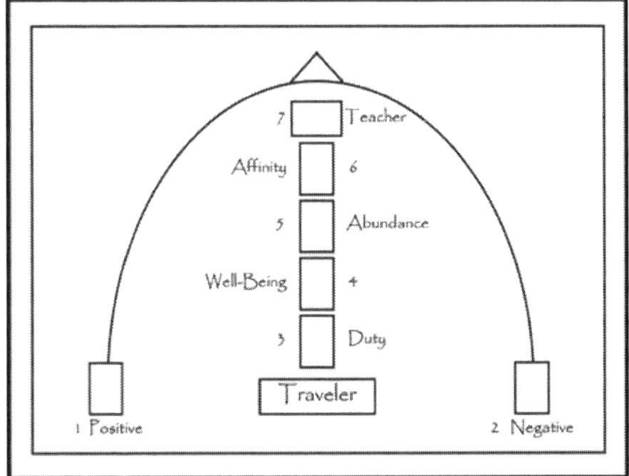


J. Dyanne looked up from the spread and grinned.

"And I thought working in Alderman Weaver's office would be boring."

I don't know why she seemed so excited.

She had The Linkboy in the negative position, opposed to Purpose in the positive. This could mean someone was trying to block her progress. And in this instance, it would be her Duty to fight like the Warrior card which landed third.

The fourth, fifth and sixth cards proved she would have the support of Courage, Spirit and the Caretaker, respectively, but, it was clear her greatest responsibility was to keep in mind the message represented by the final card in the Teacher position – Awareness.

Well, that would explain it. For J. Dyanne this would mean she'd need to keep her powers of observation heightened. In her mind, that could only point to yet another opportunity to solve a mystery.

## Chapter 12 -
## The Unexpected Relative

After school the next day, we got off the bus a stop early at Vincennes and headed to Alderman Weaver's office. The receptionist buzzed us into what Mom would have called an elegant space. The reception desk was a dark, polished wood and a large brass nameplate read "Alderman James Everett Weaver, 51st Ward, Chicago, Illinois." There was no sign for the receptionist's name. The walls were wood-paneled from the middle of the wall to the floor. The top of the walls were painted a deep navy blue, which set off the gold lettering announcing again, that this was the 51st Ward Office of Alderman James Everett Weaver.

"Good afternoon, and welcome to the offices of Alderman James Weaver. You must be our new Jr. Alderman, Jacqueléne Dyanne Dubois and your little sister, Katrin. I'm Miss Reynolds. I'll alert the Alderman that you have arrived. You can take a seat right over there."

This was all spoken without pause in an unnaturally precise tone. I recognized it as the professional tone Mom used when she picked up the phone. She could be scolding us about emptying the garbage one minute and pick up a ringing phone and shift, smooth as silk, into the 'phone voice.' I wondered how the receptionist sounded when she was with her friends.

Miss Reynolds was not an unattractive woman; she just seemed unimaginative about her appearance. She looked to be in her late twenties. Her makeup did nothing to enhance the golden highlights in her brown skin tone. And her hair was styled in a stiff flip that didn't complement her bone structure at all. I recognized the three-quarter sleeve, shirt-waist dress from one of Mom's sewing patterns, but Miss Reynolds could have used a more vibrant color than the bland, brownish-beige cotton she'd chosen. Perhaps she thought it was professional. In any case, she buzzed Weaver on the intercom and then led us back to his office.

The Honorable Alderman James Everett Weaver came forward to greet us as we entered – there was another, smaller nameplate on his very impressive desk. It was very clear that Weaver really liked being an alderman. As stylish as his secretary was plain, he wore a navy Nehru jacket today over a crisp white shirt, a triangle of gray silk peeping out of his breast pocket. The crease in his matching gray trousers was sharp as a knife.

"Welcome, welcome. Always happy to welcome young people to the inner workings of government. Please, have a seat." There were two soft leather chairs in front of the desk. "Miss Reynolds, that will be all for today. I'll be in the downtown office tomorrow. Oh, and please call Warren. I'll be ready for the car in about an hour."

"Fine, Alderman. Good night." Miss Reynolds closed the door and Weaver crossed back to his desk.

"Well girls, today I'll give you a little overview of what I do here and how the great City of Chicago works, and we'll just get to know each other a little better." I could sense that J. Dyanne was not so comfortable with all this. Naturally, she wanted the best grade she could get in Social Studies, but I could see she wasn't too pleased to be working with the man who accused her of "seeing things" last summer. Apparently, Weaver sensed it too.

"Jacqueléne, I'd like to apologize to you if anything I said last August hurt your feelings. I was just a bit on edge that day." He rose from behind the desk and crossed over to us. "You know, I understand how gifted you are." He leaned forward. "We're related in that way." He held J. Dyanne's gaze for a moment before straightening up.

I have to say, I was stunned. J. Dyanne looked incredulous. Weaver continued.

"I was very pleased when your vice principal, Mrs. Dwyer called me about this assignment. Since the August incident, I've wanted to help you... let's see, navigate the world with your talents."

"I have a caretaker. I'm just here to learn about city government."

"And so you will. And you will also learn how your talents can support a future career in politics." As a reporter, I had to speak up.

"What's your talent?" Weaver took my notebook and laid it on his desk.

"Off the record, let me just say that I have a high sensitivity to people's emotions and states of mind."

He paused for a moment, looking down at his hands. For a moment, my sense of suspicion began to lessen, started to loosen its grip on my mind. It was unnerving. I pushed back. Weaver looked up and smiled.

"Very good. Usually people don't sense when I share their feelings."

"Or try to change them," I stated.

"You can do that?" J. Dyanne asked. "Not just feel people's emotions, but change the way they feel?"

"Trust me, in politics, it's important to be able to calm tense situations in order to get things done. I share this with you because I want you to be comfortable about allowing your talents to be open while you're here. In fact, I'd be very grateful if you'd be willing to actively use your talents in support of the work here in the 51st Ward."

"What can I do?"

"From what I saw with the Ingle situation, you're good at solving mysteries, a detective with special talents. Those skills will come in handy in my work for our district. I think you'd be surprised at the number of politicians who seek advice from talents such as yourself, in both local and national politics. And you'll gain the respect you deserve, instead of silly girls like Patrice Kirkwood calling you names."

Weaver was very persuasive.

J. Dyanne was sold.

I was worried.

As we moved into October, J. Dyanne blossomed in the expression of her talent. We rode all over the city in Weaver's car, driven by the handsome Warren Murphy. Weaver took us to City Hall and the Civic Center. J. Dyanne was enthralled by the recently installed Picasso sculpture in The Civic Center Plaza. She said it reminded her of what she felt like after a vision passed through her. For me, it sometimes looked like a monkey or a gazelle. That's art for you. We sat in on meetings and afterward J. Dyanne shared her considerable insights on colleagues, city resolutions and proposed budget items. She was in her element.

She even got Miss Reynolds fired. This was on purpose, as she exposed Reynolds for skimming from the office petty cash. Alderman Weaver didn't believe it at first. He was willing to give Reynolds a second chance. But his political advisors agreed with J. Dyanne and Miss Reynolds was history. Weaver seemed really upset about the whole situation and even went so far as to promise Miss Reynolds he would do what he could to help her find another position.

I wondered if this was just a politician's promise that would go unfulfilled or if he really meant it.

The full story was a popular article in the next issue of the Nightingale Gazette.

The school year was off to a great start. J. Dyanne was acing Social Studies and the whispers, both at school and in the neighborhood were dying down.

We almost got through October without any trouble. Almost.

# Chapter 13 - A Dark and Stormy Afternoon

October 1968

Not many people know about this incident. It's something neither of us felt needed to be broadcast. But again, people tend to make up stuff that's even more outrageous if left to themselves, so I'll chronicle it here. There is no real evidence that the following ever happened. No scientific evidence that is. But it did happen.

Trust me.

It was late afternoon. The gusting winds near October's end stripped the trees of their last, fragile, faintly crimson leaves. The howling rush of wind set the windows shuddering; drafts of brisk air snaked through minute cracks. We were able to work on personal projects now that we had completed our Apollo assignments. Mr. Gordon became obsessed whenever there was a space flight. He assigned all of his Science classes from sixth through eighth grade the creation of NASA Notebooks. We were to clip articles and photos from the newspapers leading up to lift-off, continuing through the mission and the final splashdown, paste them onto notepaper and place them in a folder. This time it was Apollo 7, which orbited earth.

Collecting enough clippings wasn't always easy. Since J. Dyanne and I both had the same assignment, it meant buying extra newspapers, which wasn't always in the family budget. We had to go around the neighborhood collecting bottles to return to the store for the refund. But we got through it. Splashdown had been the week before on J. Dyanne's birthday, which brought its own surprises.

For years she was convinced that our parents habitually forgot the day she was born. Then remembering at the last minute, Mom baked a hasty cake and/or gave her a gift of whatever was handy. If this was indeed the case – which I personally doubted – this year worked out just fine. A 35mm Nikon camera. Not just any Nikon, either. J. Dyanne had coveted Dad's camera since she was a child. Now, at 13 years old, he had finally given in, deciding she was mature enough to truly appreciate it.

Today, we had covered the dining room table with our various projects. I was working on the creation of a dramatic Halloween ensemble: Scheherazade, the story-teller from the Arabian Nights. But the weather was tempting me to rethink this idea. Chicago in October is not what you'd call a sultry desert oasis.

J. Dyanne sat opposite working with extreme concentration on an aspect of her birthday present. She was determined to master the art of developing her own photographs. Of course, there are more modern methods, but the traditional way was always a fascination to us both, especially for J. Dyanne.

She would spend hours with Dad in his home-made darkroom and watch the images emerge from blankness. From a plain white sheet, first the outline, shades of gray, dark and light would mysteriously coalesce into the Chicago skyline or the hound, Dog, tearing into his food bowl. J. Dyanne was drawn to puzzles of any kind, and photography lent itself to her natural need for balance, composition, science and math. This is where I parted ways with her interests.

At the moment, her hands were buried in a kind of black, vinyl muff. Not to keep her hands warm, but a changing bag – a lightproof pouch containing exposed film. She had taken her camera on a field trip to City Hall with Alderman Weaver. We had detoured over to Buckingham Fountain and took some shots there. I was looking forward to seeing the images she captured, as I had done some amateur modeling in front of the fountain. Everybody does it.

J. Dyanne's face was a study in focus while her hands deftly loaded the unseen film onto the unseen reel and into the unseen developing tank. Her concentration was broken by the arrival of the delinquent, Derek Fremont, who lived three houses down. The only good thing I could say about him was that he was a decent softball player. He'd just turned thirteen and seemed to grow an inch every week. He was able to avoid wearing 'high water' jeans by conveniently taking over the civilian wardrobe of his elder brother, currently on a tour of duty in the Navy. The downside was Derek's new height made him think he was cooler than everybody else. He wasn't. He was what Mom called 'one of the alley people.'

Dad often had the garage door open while working on his motorcycle and folks would stroll by and start talking. Young, old, mostly of the male gender. But they all eventually gathered around that alley-side garage door, drawn like moths to the light that was Mr. Dubois. He was a wise talker, and more important, a wise listener. Even the delinquents respected and listened to him.

It seemed the chill, rushing wind didn't stop some of them. Rumor had it that Derek's brother, Troy, was AWOL from the Navy. Apparently all the Fremonts were delinquents. Perhaps Dad had some wise words of comfort for him.

Derek had come into the house, ostensibly, for a drink of water. Why he needed to interrupt our endeavors was a mystery to me. Except that he always felt the need to taunt J. Dyanne.

He sauntered into the room as if he expected us to be thrilled to see him. By way of greeting, he raised his fist in the air, imitating the Black Power salute gold medalist Tommie Smith used in last week's Olympics. Barely glancing at me, he went into immediate taunting mode.

"Hey, Jacks, what're you doing? Polishing your crystal ball?" Fortunately for her, J. Dyanne had the ability to completely ignore anyone she found annoying or stupid. I did not possess this gift.

"If you must know," I ventured, "she's preparing exposed film for developing. As if it's any of your business."

He wasn't listening. He was taunting.

"Jackalini, Jackasprini, what're you gonna be for Halloweenie," he cackled. He really was annoying. But what do you expect? He was a boy.

J. Dyanne completed threading the film and removed the developing tank from the bag. As she reached for the next roll, Derek snatched it up.

With the heaviest of sighs, J. Dyanne leaned back in her chair.

"Katrin, it seems there's a poltergeist in the house." With an air of supreme indifference, she picked up an unmarked, brown bottle.

"Call in the hound?"

"The Male Teen Elder might help," I replied. J. Dyanne looked thoughtfully at the bottle in her hand.

"Of course, I could always use the photo acid." I knew it was simply rubbing alcohol, but it caught Derek's attention. He reached over and placed a roll of film on the table. J. Dyanne hesitated.

"What's that?"

Derek tried looking innocent. I was confused, until I looked more closely. J. Dyanne had been using Kodak, distinctive in its bright yellow canister. On the table was a green and white canister... I could just make out the name "Fuji" on its side. I was beginning to be quite annoyed on J. Dyanne's behalf, but a slight signal from her stopped my hasty words. She turned to Derek.

"Tell me," she said.

He fidgeted a bit, hands in pocket, then out. Finally coming to grips with some inner demon, he rubbed his close-cropped hair and relaxed. With a sincerity I had never seen in him before, he told us.

"That..." indicating the Fuji film, "was sent to me in the mail. From my brother."

"What was the post mark?"

"Mexico. There was a note, not much, just saying he thought I'd like to see Mexico, and he didn't have time to write more."

"Why bring it to me? You can get this developed anywhere."

He fidgeted some more, then sat at the table.

"Look, I don't have the money to get it developed, and I didn't want to ask my mom... I don't know what he might have put on there." I quickly caught on.

"So, there might be some stupid girly pictures you don't want your mom to see, huh?" He looked at me with a sly grin.

"Maybe. He's seeing the world and there're a lot of girls out there." J. Dyanne brought us back to the point.

"So, you want me to develop it for you, in case there's something incriminating? Why would I do that? This is between you and your brother," she said, pushing the film aside. Derek pushed it back, anxiety now crowded his eyes.

"No, wait. Listen, I think it might have something to do with where he is." Now he had J. Dyanne's interest.

"Go on," she said.

"The date on the note was the day before he was reported AWOL. And I know something must have happened. He would no sooner be absent without leave than... than you'd go out with me."

"Maybe his tour of duty changed his mind and he wanted out."

"Okay, so he didn't much like being in Vietnam, but Troy loved being in the Navy. He's dreamed about it since he was a kid. Anyway, Mr. D. said he taught you how to develop pics, so maybe you could... you know, you could do these."

J. Dyanne didn't immediately respond. She looked intrigued, though I was suspicious. I didn't trust Derek Fremont. He was probably hoping to trick us with some pictures of a really gross Halloween trick.

"Look," Derek continued. "Something happened... something made him disappear. And maybe there's something in these pictures to give me a clue."

He'd said the magic word... J. Dyanne loved searching out clues to mysteries. Personally, I thought it was a lost cause, but then I wasn't counting on the unique abilities of Jacqueléne Dyanne.

# Chapter 14 - Developments

J. Dyanne meticulously lined up her tools – changing bag, scissors, film picker, developing canister and lid, film reel and stem. She deftly pulled the film leader from the canister with the film picker, and with precision, rounded the corners of the film with small snips of the scissors. Satisfied that the film would easily load onto the reel, she placed all she needed into the changing bag – film, reel and stem and developing canister – and went to work.

For a moment Derek looked a bit nervous.

"She does know what she's doing, right?"

I gave him what I hoped was a withering glance. "Of course," I snapped. "Shhh..."

J. Dyanne was done in record time. She withdrew her hands from the bag, unzipped the end, pulled out the now full developing canister and headed for the tiny darkroom Dad had built next to the bathroom. We got up to follow, but were halted in our tracks.

"I need to concentrate. You're too distracting."

I knew this was the tricky part. Get the chemicals right, pour the developer, fixer and stop bath at the right time, the right temperature and right order. I had often joined J. Dyanne during this process, but realized that Derek would definitely be in the way. So, I calmly agreed. Even though that meant I was left alone with the delinquent. What does one say to such a person?

"This will take some time. You should probably leave. Come back later. Or tomorrow," I said hopefully. It was no surprise when he declined.

I returned to my task, hoping Derek would become bored and go away. He did get bored, however without J. Dyanne to taunt he turned his unfortunate attentions to me. I was sewing the hem to the veil of my Scheherazade costume. Derek apparently couldn't resist being annoying or stand being ignored.

"What's that?"

"A veil, if you must know," I snapped.

"What're you going to be, the Bride of Frankenstein?" He laughed as though he'd been quite clever. Really, he was such a juvenile.

"If you must know--"

"I must! I must!" he interrupted.

"I'm going to be Scheherazade, and this is--" He was laughing again.

"Stop it! You don't even know who that is."

"Sure, I do. She's the one who told all the stories so the king wouldn't kill her." I looked at him in blank surprise.

"You're not the only person who reads," he quipped.

"So, what's so funny?" I insisted. He snatched

up the finished harem pants and began to sashay around the room.

"She's supposed to be fine as wine and you're--" He broke off and quickly tossed the pants aside. Dad had entered the room.

"Uh, hey Mr. D" he croaked. Dad gave him a piercing look and solemnly nodded.

"Young man," he intoned and slowly went upstairs.

I recognized this maneuver as one Dad often used when the Female Teen Elder Other had a date visiting. It wasn't unnecessarily intrusive and he simply walked through the room. But it put the boy on guard that indeed, he was being watched and had better behave. Dad would come back downstairs in a few minutes, 'cause really, there wasn't that much to do up there. But it was reassuring to know he was around.

Before Derek could return to his silliness, J. Dyanne re-appeared.

"You'll want to see this," she said, and turned back to the darkroom.

I dropped my sewing, and managed to enter the darkroom before Derek. It wasn't that big a space and so we barely fit. It had been a linen closet before Dad converted it. I stood next to J. Dyanne and Derek squeezed in on my other side. The familiar chemical smell was almost overpowered by Derek's cologne, but not quite. The combination was a bit nauseating. In the dim reddish light, J. Dyanne held up a contact sheet showing a small image of each photo on the roll.

"Definitely Mexico. Obviously Tijuana, as you can see in this shot of Troy and some other sailors posing in front of the city sign. It gets more interesting here." She pointed to the last few pictures on the sheet.

"There's Troy, one of his buddies and this Mexican woman."

"Yeah, that's Troy and Gus... Gustavo Villareal" Derek said with a flourish. "Cool name, huh? His family's from Mexico, but he was born in Arizona. They were in boot camp together, got assigned the same ship."

"What's so significant about these, Dyanne?"

"You'll see in a minute. I'm making 8x10's."

A timer sounded. J. Dyanne took the exposed print paper from the enlarger and placed it in the developer tray. We watched the images form of two men, Troy and Gus, flanking a woman, who looked at Gus with an amazing intensity. Once the images were clear, J. Dyanne removed it with the tongs and slid the paper into the stop bath, which ended the development cycle and then into the fixer tray to seal the image and finally the wash to clear off any residual chemicals. She repeated the procedure twice more, hanging each complete photo to dry with a wooden clothespin.

The darkroom had become very stuffy by this time, what with its small size, the smells and the three of us crammed in there. I wanted to open the door but couldn't reach it with Derek in the way. I started to ask him to move when something in the photo caught my eye.

"What's that they're holding?"

"Skulls," said J. Dyanne. "If I'm not mistaken those are traditional sugar skulls in honor of the Day of the Dead."

"*Calaveras de azucar en honor del Día de los Muertos*," said Derek. We both stared at him.

"I'm taking Spanish, so what?" He looked at J. Dyanne. "But Day of the Dead isn't till after Halloween."

"Actually, some places begin before Halloween, also known as All Hallow's Eve and continue through November 2nd, All Soul's Day."

The depth of J. Dyanne's knowledge on obscure subjects always amazed me. It must be all the reading.

"However," she continued, "preparation for Day of the Dead can begin quite a while before Halloween. The holiday not only celebrates those who have passed on, it is also believed that at this time, the veil separating the living and the dead is lifted and souls can communicate directly with those still living."

Looking more closely at the photos, it appeared Troy was in some kind of marketplace. In the background were carts and shop windows filled with skeleton dolls, skulls, candles and miniature caskets. J. Dyanne was pointing to the pictures.

"Marigolds, *flor de muertos*, special bread, *pan de muerto*. Those mini caskets are made of cake or marzipan. Altars or *ofrendas* are set up in homes, or even in the cemetery. Everything is geared to celebrate and communicate with the departed.

Some people stay up all night hoping their loved ones will return in answer to their prayers."

I have to say, this was all new to me and I wasn't sure I liked it. Or maybe it was just the stuffiness in the room. But I was curious.

"Dyanne, why these three photos?

"Look here, just at the edge of the frame?"

There was a small figure of a boy staring blankly into the camera. He wasn't Mexican; he looked darker, and in fact looked like a younger version of Derek. The boy wasn't part of the shot. But looking closely at all three photos, which were taken in different locations, this same boy was in all of them. The final photo was just Gus and the woman. She was feeding him one of the sugar skulls. I was about to comment on this, when I'm quite sure the boy in the photo... *waved.* I blinked to clear my vision and upon opening my eyes saw, to my absolute astonishment, that next to the boy... although it was clearly impossible... but next to the boy in the photo, stood J. Dyanne. I stared and blinked once more. Obviously, I needed some air or something. But, when I opened my eyes once again, I was no longer looking at the photo.

I was in it.

# Chapter 15 - Día de los Muertos

At first, I couldn't breathe. The air was much too thin. My body felt like a paper doll and every figure, building and tree was like a two-dimensional cutout. A single, forced breath was dragged into my lungs and everything popped into life. Sound jumped into my ears along with wild laughter, unfamiliar music, strange instruments and singing. And although it was night, it was not the black and white world of the photo. Light, bright color cascaded all around like a nightmare in Technicolor. Skulls, tombstones, skeletons dressed in brightly colored dresses and tuxedoes, yellow flowers, and lights... so many lights. Breathing more deeply, the crazy universe in which I'd landed came into focus.

It was then I realized I was clutching Derek's arm. He too had been drawn into this photo-phantasmagorical world. I immediately removed my hand. The sound was fading but still just a bit too raucous and loud. Apparently we had arrived in the train of a rowdy procession. A group of what looked like dancing ghouls was trailing behind a crowd carrying a coffin filled with bright marigolds.

J. Dyanne looked less amazed and more intrigued. After all, this was indeed a unique situation in which we found ourselves. Derek got his bearings and, seeing his brother, reached for him. It was like watching a hand float through mist. He jumped back with a yelp of surprise. The figures of Troy, Gus and the woman carried on without any awareness of our presence.

But then there was the boy from the photo. He turned to us.

"Thanks for coming," he said casually. J. Dyanne studied him intently.

"Why are we here?" she asked.

"There are ways you can help."

"How? They don't even see us."

The boy smiled. "There are many ways of communicating. Follow me."

"Follow you? Who are you?" Derek demanded. "How did we get here? What's going on?"

The boy looked at him. There was something sad in his smile, but not unkind.

"You can trust me Derek. I'm here to help you and Troy." I wondered how he knew Derek's name.

"What have you done with my brother? Where is he?"

I didn't blame Derek for being upset, but this didn't seem to be the time to antagonize the only person who could possibly make sense of what was happening. I intervened.

"Excuse me, but what's your name? Have we met before?"

The boy looked at me with the same kindly and sad smile.

"Alexander. My mom always thought I was going to be something great. And no, we haven't met before. At least not like this."

I didn't understand what he meant, but J. Dyanne had a knowing look on her face.

"Do you know what this is about?" I asked her.

She looked from Alexander to Derek and back.

"I'll explain later. Let's just trust Alexander and get going."

And with a sound like a shutter click from a camera we jumped into the next frame. I didn't recognize this scene and realized we had moved beyond the roll of film Troy had sent.

There wasn't a lot of light here or music. Candles flickered at a few sparsely decorated graves. There were headstones and what looked like small houses. A figure moved up ahead. This time it was Derek who grabbed my arm. J. Dyanne and Alexander maneuvered through the headstones toward one of the tiny house-like shrines. I again shook free from Derek and followed. I wasn't about to be left alone with only him for company.

Running toward the light in the shrine, I heard something rustling and turned to find Troy sneaking toward the same place. He never got there. As he passed a tall stone angel, a white-cloaked figure seemed to float up from the outstretched wings, an arm raised to strike. My call of warning was unheard by Troy as the arm swung out swiftly knocking him down and out. Someone came out of the shrine. It was the woman from earlier. She and the white-cloaked attacker picked up Troy and carried him inside.

Alexander beckoned us forward. I began to tiptoe, and then remembered they couldn't hear or see us. Feeling slightly unnerved, I ran ahead. There were letters carved in the stone over the door. I didn't waste time trying to make them out. We crowded inside. The sight was amazing.

Gus was already there. He was surrounded by flowers, candles, bottles of tequila, platters of candied pumpkins and tamales, *pan de muerto*, a box of cigars, all laid out on what could only be what J. Dyanne had called an *ofrenda*, an elaborate altar. In the middle of the altar was a wooden cross overhanging a framed photo of the woman and a man who looked a lot like Gus. The actual Gus was gagged and tied to a chair, alive but not looking so well. Especially when he saw Troy being carried in and laid in a corner of the shrine. The hood of the white-cloaked figure fell back. An older woman's face was revealed as she pointed, with barely suppressed excitement, to the altar. Fluttering over the candles was a brightly colored Monarch butterfly.

The old woman spoke. "See Monica, your husband's soul has indeed returned."

J. Dyanne responded to my look of utter confusion.

"Monarch butterflies return to Mexico from the north during the time of *Día de los Muertos*. It's believed they carry the spirits of the departed."

She looked at Monica, who was looking at Gus with the same frightening intensity I'd seen in one of the photos.

"Apparently, they think Monica's husband has returned in both spirit and body. Notice the similarity between Gus and the man in the photo."

I could see the resemblance, but I was no closer to understanding why they had captured Gus. We were soon to find out and it wasn't for a picnic.

"But what has my brother got to do with this?"

Alexander spoke. "Gus is Troy's shipmate. He couldn't abandon him. Troy had to find him. That's why he's AWOL."

Perhaps Troy wasn't a delinquent after all.

"What... what are they going to do with him?" Derek whispered.

No one spoke. It seemed kind of obvious. Then Monica, who had knelt next to Gus, spoke.

"Thank you, Alejandro... thank you for hearing my prayers. I will go back with you. On the day of souls, death will unite us instead of tearing us apart."

This did not sound good at all. I felt dizzy. The crowded space, the smell of incense and candles, the scent of the marigolds was suffocating. In the light, my vision blurred, but it wasn't the light, it was the butterflies. There were dozens of them now, sweeping over the *ofrenda*, throughout the shrine, dozens and dozens of them, their wings fluttering in a sudden rush of wind. And suddenly, there was no air.

# Chapter 16 - Absent Without Leave

A long deep breath drew up through my chest and the world popped into focus. Fluttering overhead were butterflies, but then I realized it was Mom waving a magazine over my face. I wasn't in the darkroom, but lay out on the living room couch. J. Dyanne was sitting up in an armchair and Derek was sitting on the floor. His Mom had arrived and was kneeling next to him. Dad was opening windows, letting in the crisp autumn air. I noticed the wind had died down with nightfall. I took another deep breath. Mom looked worried, so I smiled up at her. Her face relaxed for a moment and then returned to a familiar *mater familias* stern and annoyed look.

"How many times do we have to tell you? Turn on the ventilator when you're developing!"

"Sorry. I forgot," J. Dyanne murmured. We had, it seemed, briefly passed out from the fumes of the developer. Dad knelt next to J. Dyanne's chair.

"From now on, you check with me or your mother before you go in there again, understand?" J. Dyanne nodded.

"I promise," she said.

I looked over to her. The three prints she had developed were clutched in her hand. Silently, she handed them to me.

The photos looked the same, except Alexander wasn't in any of them. There was just a flare of light where he had previously appeared.

I sat up, a little too quickly as I was still a bit dizzy. But I was so surprised it didn't matter. I handed them to Derek. He was just as dazed and for once, silent. Mrs. Fremont now gazed down at the photos.

"Where did you get these? When were these taken?"

"Troy sent them to me. I was hoping they would help us figure out what happened to him."

"Dad," J. Dyanne began, "Derek's brother is in trouble. He's lost down in Mexico. In Tijuana." She snatched the pictures from Derek. "There isn't much time. Alexander showed us the cemetery." She turned quickly to Mrs. Fremont who had gasped. "They're alive. But they're stuck in a shrine. The family name is Moreno... that's the name carved over the doorway. The woman who trapped them is Monica... Monica Moreno. We've only got until Nov. 2nd, All Soul's Day... the Day of the Dead. She's waiting till then. That's less than a week away."

Derek was looking at J. Dyanne in a whole new light. I could tell he wouldn't be taunting her any time soon. Mrs. Fremont was also staring at her, transfixed.

"Who is Alexander?"

"You wouldn't believe it if we told you," Derek murmured.

"Try me. I've heard about you," she said pointing at J. Dyanne. "And I think... just tell me."

J. Dyanne rarely enjoyed speaking about herself, so I explained about the boy that used to be in the photo and our experience in Tijuana. I expected Mrs. Fremont to tell the parents to have me put away or toss off the story as delirium from the chemicals. But she simply reached for a locket she wore around her neck and opened it.

"Was this the boy?"

We looked at the photo inside, and there he was, a happily smiling Alexander. J. Dyanne moved to sit on the floor next to Mrs. Fremont.

"How old was he when he died?"

Mrs. Fremont smiled a sad, but kindly smile. Just like Alexander's.

"He was only seven. He'd be almost 30 now. He was our firstborn. After he died we tried again for the longest time, and then years later, we had Troy and then Derek."

Now it was Derek's turn to stare at his mom.

"You mean I had another brother? And you never told me?"

"He was from another part of my life. I didn't want to burden you with that kind of pain."

"Mrs. Fremont?" J. Dyanne said. "You know, souls never die. And he's still living up to his name. It's a great thing to come back and help his little brother. It's what you named him for, right?"

This time, Mrs. Fremont's smile was happy.

"Yes, he is Alexander the Great." She turned to the parents. "So, let's get moving. Your daughter says we've got less than a week."

Mom and Dad almost collectively breathed a heavy sigh. J. Dyanne had presented them with yet another unusual task. But that's what you can expect when you have a daughter like Jacqueléne Dyanne.

* * *

We enlisted the help of Alderman Weaver to find Troy and Gus. You'd think it would be a politician's dream... help save the hero son of a local voter. I don't mean to sound cynical, but we had to do some convincing. Weaver was worried about associating with anything not easily explained. After all his talk about being open to J. Dyanne's talents, he was certainly backtracking about the possibility of going public. But Dad calmly explained that Weaver could assert his influence by simply saying Derek received a communication that placed Troy in Mexico. The photos could identify the general area and he wouldn't have to mention anything about J. Dyanne's talents. He finally agreed. But not before his friendly luster faded in J. Dyanne's eyes.

There was nothing more we could do except wait for news. Which fortunately turned out good. With the help of Mrs. Fremont and the photos developed by J. Dyanne, the Mexican authorities were able to follow the trail to the cemetery from the last photo taken and found Troy and Gus in time.

The woman, Monica was put under psychiatric care. It seems she had been a newlywed when her husband, Alejandro had died several months earlier in an accident. She was having a hard time coming to terms with the grief. They never found her mother.

As I said before, there is no scientific evidence that any of this happened, but it did. In fact, I still have the sugar skull that somehow found its way into the pocket of my jeans.

J. Dyanne was in a very pensive mood on *Día de los Muertos*. I ventured to ask what was on her mind. She looked out at the autumn leaves racing along the sidewalk.

"Love and loss," she said. "It can do odd things to the mind."

This I believed. For instance, the delinquent, Derek Fremont, had been very distant with us lately. Not that I was complaining. But it seemed to me that J. Dyanne was feeling the self-consciousness of being perceived as different. After Derek, an outsider, had such a close encounter with whatever it was that made J. Dyanne unusual, he'd stopped coming around to taunt and seemed almost afraid to even look at her. I guess it comes with the territory when you're different, but it can't always feel so good. When I mentioned this to J. Dyanne, she merely looked amused.

"Oh, I'm not worried about Derek," she chuckled. "He's not part of *my* future." Well, he certainly wasn't going to be part of mine, so I didn't know why she was looking at me in that 'oh I know something you don't know' kind of way.

What I think worried her more was the near-defection of Alderman Weaver. When he heard the full story, he seemed more wary of having J. Dyanne around. A little bit of talent was okay, but something as strong as what J. Dyanne was exhibiting seemed too much for him to handle. Or maybe he felt her talents were something he couldn't control. As it was, I didn't like to see J. Dyanne so withdrawn. But this was not my greatest concern.

It was the math that really had me worried.

# Chapter 17 - Logic Rules

November 1968

Several weeks had passed since our foray into Derek's photo-phantasmagorical world. J. Dyanne's talents had saved the two sailors, but apparently this was at a personal price. That price was an incessant pre-occupation with math – and not just rudimentary numbers and equations.

It was deeper trouble than that.

J. Dyanne had become obsessed with word problems. The most worrisome feature of this state of mind is that she felt it necessary to share these "entertainments" with me.

Conversations all too frequently began with variations of the dreaded "If a train left the station at 10:00am going 85 miles per hour..." This was especially painful for me, because I did not feel that perfectly good words should be put to such base use. But to J. Dyanne these puzzles had a soothing, calming, even healing effect upon her psyche. And her psyche needed a lot of healing.

After the energy expended with Alexander, I noticed that her sleep was consistently restless and she would not discuss her dreams, if there were any to discuss. And she refused to take part in our study of the Wisdom Cards.

School, math and logic were her refuge. The new math teacher was actually pretty good, so in the scholastic realm, J. Dyanne was doing fine. In other ways, she had closed down. I imagine this was a protective action.

I was writing regular stories for the Nightingale Elementary Gazette and J. Dyanne submitted great photos. She was rarely seen without her camera. And she was still as efficient as ever in her work with Alderman Weaver.

However, there was clearly strain in their working relationship. This was exacerbated when Weaver discovered that J. Dyanne no longer utilized her talents. He didn't want anything wild, but she had been very useful to him before. He was unnerved by the shift. Admittedly, J. Dyanne's normal acuity was above average for even most adults and her keen observational skills were very much in full force and still proved useful.

I believe Weaver's primary concern was his realization that his own talents could not read her. I could tell when he tried. The energy just rolled past her like a cool breeze. But we were on this assignment until Thanksgiving, so Weaver kept us busy.

After all the drama of the Democratic Convention, Election Day came and Hubert Humphrey lost out to Richard Milhous Nixon. Surprisingly, Alderman Weaver took heart with the Republican win... he thought that maybe he could shift things in Chicago, like maybe he could be mayor. He was a Democrat, but toyed with the idea of going over to the other side. His advisors though convinced him to try and build his public profile as a Democrat. Maybe try organizing some community things like that young Black Panther leader, Fred Hampton. Breakfast programs, gang peace treaties... things like that. Chicago wouldn't soon go Republican. I think he was able to sense our discomfort with his opportunist leanings.

"It's all politics," Weaver explained. "You do what you have to do in order to serve the people best."

I wasn't buying it. And neither was J. Dyanne. My reading of the Wisdom Cards consistently brought up the Linkboy, often in the cautionary position. Naturally, Derek was my first suspect, but it was becoming increasingly more obvious the card pointed to Weaver.

Soon, the cusp of the holiday season was upon us. The days were uniformly gray with the occasional blast of brilliant autumn sunlight that added gilt highlights to the burnt oranges and reds of tree-lined Winthrop Avenue. It was one of those bright days that once again shifted our focus.

For the school Science Fair, my entry was a three-dimensional model of the human heart. I got the idea from the one at the Museum of Science and Industry where you could actually walk inside all the chambers. Mine would be on a much smaller scale, of course. J. Dyanne was creating a model of a smoking volcano. We had walked over to the Ace Hardware to buy poster boards on which to illustrate our diagrams and findings. Leaving the store, J. Dyanne suddenly pushed me back against the wall and peered around the edge of the building. Next door was the back entrance to Weaver's office and there was the former receptionist, Miss Reynolds, unlocking the door. Once she was inside, we crossed to the entrance of the alley. We waited out of sight from the office but where we still had a clear view of the door.

"What could she want? Do you think she's stealing something?"

J. Dyanne didn't respond. She just pulled out her camera. A few minutes later, Miss Reynolds came out as a car pulled up to the door. It was Warren in Alderman Weaver's car. What could they be up to? Reynolds was already fired. Was Warren an accomplice? I hoped not. He was nice. But I couldn't figure out what it all meant.

J. Dyanne developed the film that day. And yes, we got permission first. On Tuesday we showed up, as usual, after school.

The new receptionist, Mrs. Walker, could have won a Coretta Scott King look-a-like contest, with her perfectly styled hair and makeup. Her matronly figure was clothed in a maroon, double-breasted suit dress, accessorized with a triple strand necklace of silver beads. Very professional, I thought. Plus, she was much more friendly than Miss Reynolds. She buzzed us in and directed us right into Weaver's office.

"Good afternoon, ladies," he said. "We've got a lot to do today. Mrs. Walker has some correspondence that needs filing."

J. Dyanne simply placed the photos on his desk.

Weaver looked over the photos and then at J. Dyanne, with what I'm sure he hoped was innocent curiosity.

"What is this?"

"That's what we'd like to know, too."

Weaver looked again at the photo. "I assume this is a picture of Warren giving Miss Reynolds a ride home. He often did so when she worked here."

"These were taken yesterday," I said. Weaver appeared to study the pictures again.

"I'm not sure I understand... unless... oh, I see. Well," he smiled broadly. "Thank you. Thank you for bringing this to my attention. I mean one could assume that there was some wrong-doing going on here, as Miss Reynolds no longer works here. But the thing is... you say this was yesterday?" J. Dyanne nodded. "Then I know exactly what happened. Miss Reynolds still had a few personal belongings here and I asked Warren to drive her over and turn in her key." He pushed the photos across the desk.

"So, if that's all, why don't you get started on that filing?" I turned to leave, but J. Dyanne gave one last, searching look at Weaver before moving away.

"Oh, and by the way, Jacqueléne, I'll be giving my final report to your vice principal this week. I'm sure you'll receive a very nice grade with all the extra credit points from your work here."

Oh, he was smooth all right. He figured a subtle

threat about our grades would keep us quiet about what may or may not have happened with Miss Reynolds. That day we did our work and went home. But it wasn't over yet.

Soon we were to embark on the annual four-day Thanksgiving holiday. Looking back I, but more to the point J. Dyanne, should have recognized the first hint that something unusual was at play. We had completed our day of scholastic pursuits and were awaiting the cream and green limousine, otherwise known as the Chicago Transit Authority bus. We might be lucky and find the driver was one of our many DuBois cousins, Turk. Instead, as we boarded the vehicle, a group of giggling high school girls crowded on behind us. One of them was the would-be clever extortionist, Patrice Kirkwood.

I never felt she'd forgiven J. Dyanne for exposing her plans last August to ensure her future as an NFL wife. Not only had she and football hero Paul Ingle broken up at her 17th birthday party, but she had to do community service at a homeless shelter several times a week as part of the disciplinary action for the fake kidnapping plot. I knew she couldn't stand that. And there she was sitting in the back of the bus with her friends, whispering, and I was sure, plotting something.

J. Dyanne, on the other hand, didn't notice. Not only was she pre-occupied with math problems, this was never J. Dyanne's favorite time of year. I wasn't sure if it was because she was sympathetic to the Native American point of view that for them, this holiday ultimately symbolized "Thanks-taking" or rather because it meant yet another uncomfortable family gathering. As noted, she gets crowded when the family comes together because the ancestors try to contact her with messages for the living. But all access to her intuitive right-brain universe was still numb and she was compensating by immersing herself in complete, analytical left-brain activity. I had hoped this would soon pass, but it persisted. As the holidays approached, my intuition, which was never very strong, began to quiver with unease.

I knew there were occasions when J. Dyanne wasn't completely comfortable with whatever this talent was she possessed. And over the past several weeks, it seemed she almost gleefully refuted any suggestions that she had any extra psychic ability. People had been hounding her since word got out about the Troy Fremont incident. And she kept insisting that there was nothing unusual going on, no visions, no dreams, nothing special here. It had gotten to the point where I actually had to tell J. Dyanne what I was thinking. Weird.

She was so immersed in a math puzzle, I had to practically pull her off the bus, or we would have missed our stop. And Grand Anne was expecting us.

# Chapter 18 - Patrice's Tale

As we walked from the bus stop to Yemaya I became aware of a presence. A tingling sensation crept along my neck that had nothing to do with the November wind. I quickly turned around and to my surprise saw Patrice tailing us. With J. Dyanne's sensors down, who knows what Patrice would have done if I hadn't spotted her.

"What do you want? Why are you following us?" I demanded.

"Who says I'm following you?" she quipped.

J. Dyanne held me back.

"Calm down, Katrin. It's perfectly obvious Patrice is on her way to volunteer at the homeless shelter."

As always, J. Dyanne was right. It was only three blocks from Yemaya.

"So, if you'll excuse me..." Patrice snapped and walked ahead. Suddenly, she stopped, then slowly turned toward us.

"Actually..." she began, then paused looking us over. "Can I trust you?" she blurted out.

Who was she to talk about trust? I was ready to counter, when J. Dyanne spoke up.

"What's on your mind?"

"Well, you know I don't believe in any of that psychic stuff. I mean, yes, I called you a witch and all, but seriously, it's just that you can figure things out, right?"

"Right."

"That's what I was thinking. And well, everybody knows I have to do this volunteer thing, thanks to you."

"You and Paul are the ones who tried to--" J. Dyanne shook her head. I was silenced.

"Go on," she encouraged.

Patrice took a deep breath, looked off down the street and let it all out.

She was frightened about going to the shelter. She had overheard two of the homeless men plotting to steal from the business office.

"And? Why tell me? Tell the manager. Or better yet, tell the police."

"Oh, like the police want to hear from me after last August. I'm already on probation. And the manager? Please! He thinks all those people are like suffering saints or something. He's always talking about what a shame it is that people always think the worst of them and all. He lets them work in his office, cleaning up and stuff. And they know where all the money is and the food and clothes and stuff. And now they're just gonna rip him off."

"So what's it to you?" I queried. "Don't tell me you're now a crime-buster."

"Look, if I can stop this from happening, maybe I can get my life back and never have to go back to that smelly place again. But I could use some help." She looked expectantly at J. Dyanne. But I spoke first.

"Do you have any proof of this story?" I demanded. Patrice looked at me with her lip curled.

"You're obviously not the smart one. If I had solid proof I could take care of it myself, now couldn't I? What I need to do is catch them in the act. That will be proof."

I could sense J. Dyanne being drawn into this scenario. Finally, someone was asking her to do some actual sleuthing instead of prophesizing. But then again, J. Dyanne was no dummy.

"Again, why me? You've got plenty of friends and you don't even like me."

"Got that right. But irregardless of--"

"'Irregardless' is not a real word," I prompted. "It's a double negative."

Patrice simply gave me a stony stare.

"Irregardless," she said pointedly, "of whether I like you or not, I can use your smarts." I think she knew J. Dyanne was hooked. She smiled. I didn't like it.

"You're coming to volunteer tomorrow, right? Well, that's when it's going down. Everybody who's gonna give donations will give by Thanksgiving. The place'll be loaded. We can stay to help clean up, right? And then hide and catch them."

"You plan to be there, too?" J. Dyanne asked.

"Of course. No sense in letting you get all the credit. I need to crack this so I can get outta there."

We had reached the front of the candle shop.

Grand Anne was sitting by the window and waved as we approached. Patrice looked startled.

"You know that old lady?"

"That's our grandmother, thank you," I replied.

"Oh, well, no offense, but... well, never mind. See you tomorrow." And she scurried off.

# Chapter 19 - Yemaya

It felt good to be rid of Patrice and step over the threshold of Yemaya. The fragrance of the shop immediately took me under its spell. There were rarely a lot of customers at Grand Anne's shop, and although that may have had a negative impact on sales, it made our visits so much more enjoyable.

"Is that your apple spice tea?" I asked eagerly. Grand Anne smiled and nodded. She knew it was my favorite. But one look at J. Dyanne and her expression shifted.

"You, I think, require something else, yes?" She pulled out a chair from the counter and pointed. J. Dyanne sat.

"I'm fine. Really," she insisted. Grand Anne gave one of her insistent, penetrating stares. They didn't happen often, but when they did, you were powerless. I suppose that's where *mater familias* got it from.

"Okay, so maybe I'm going through a phase or something. But honest, I'm fine," J. Dyanne insisted.

"It's all math and logic and statistics," I blurted

out. “She didn’t even know that pest was following us. I had to--”

Grand Anne held up a hand, which stopped my rant.

“I imagine what happened at Halloween was overwhelming.”

“I’m not overwhelmed.”

“Don’t interrupt. Now, it takes time to recover, but you’ve got to want to recover.” J. Dyanne didn’t answer.

“Jacqueléne? Are you going to accept it or not?” she asked.

J. Dyanne sat, drooping just a bit, as if a burden was sitting on her shoulders. Grand Anne continued.

“When you have a talent, you either use it or lose it.” J. Dyanne straightened up.

“But I have other talents,” she insisted. “They work, too. Besides, Katrin can develop hers more. Let her do it.”

I wasn’t so sure about all that. And I also wasn’t so sure I wanted to know. Grand Anne sighed and set out her porcelain tea cups.

“That remains to be seen. The question is whether you’ll be able to fulfill your part. You’ll need all your talents for that.” J. Dyanne had a few penetrating stares of her own, and, with all due respect, she put one on now. Grand Anne sighed again.

“That’s the DuBois in you, being so hard-headed,” she said. “I saw it coming, but I’d hoped... well, no sense fighting with fate. You go on and do this your way."

Once again, I was lost in the subtleties of the conversation. But apparently J. Dyanne and Grand Anne understood each other. Even with her senses down, they were able to communicate in ways other people didn't. Although this time it seemed they weren't exactly in agreement.

Then Grand Anne turned to me.

"I've got something for you." She reached into one of the jewelry displays and pulled out a necklace. It was a gemstone pendant hung with a rich, forest green ribbon. The stone was a polished greenish-gray, streaked with blue, and my favorite color, yellow. Grand Anne draped it around my neck.

"Been meaning to give you that for some time. The color suits you."

I was a bit uncomfortable. Not that I didn't like gifts. *Nequaquam*, as they say in the Latin, not at all. I loved gifts and the necklace was really nice. But it seemed that Grand Anne wasn't planning on giving anything to J. Dyanne but a hard time to go and a short time to get there.

"Hurry up now and finish your tea. I'll get your mother's package ready." With that she disappeared into the back of the shop. I turned to J. Dyanne, who was looking absently at the pendant around my neck. I can't say the look was wistful, but it was unnerving.

"You know, I bet she's got something set aside for you, too." At this, J. Dyanne grimaced.

"I'm sure she does. I just don't think I'm ready

for it." She pulled her gaze from the necklace. "Just be sure you don't lose that. Grand Anne doesn't give random gifts, you know."

Grand Anne returned with a shopping bag of dinner candles and fresh cut herbs. We were on the verge of departure when J. Dyanne asked a question.

"Grand Anne, what do you know about the shelter... Auburn Park Shelter?"

Busy collecting our tea things, Grand Anne didn't immediately answer.

"They do some good. Can't deny that. But I'd say it's not quite kosher."

"Is it the personnel or the clientele?"

Grand Anne gave J. Dyanne an appraising look.

"Well now, I imagine you'll figure all that out tomorrow, won't you?"

Like J. Dyanne, I knew Grand Anne had insights unavailable to the rest of us. And also like J. Dyanne, Grand Anne was often reticent about sharing details, preferring that mere mortals like me learn in due time as events unfolded. But knowing J. Dyanne was blocked, I was surprised Grand Anne wasn't more forthcoming. Perhaps my expectations were unrealistic. Perhaps there really was nothing to worry about. Perhaps...

# Chapter 20 - Thanksgiving

There was absolutely nothing as wonderful at this time of year than coming home to the luscious aroma created by the cooking talents of *mater familias*. She had begun preparing the Thanksgiving feast.

Our return was in time to help with the baking. Mom had started with the pies: apple, sweet potato, a peach cobbler. My favorite task during these preparations was crushing the graham crackers for the sweetened and spiced crust for the lemon meringue pie. Yes, there was a lot for which to be thankful.

Great Aunt Alis had arrived with what we called her mystery meat dish. It was a mystery because it was covered in gravy and mushrooms and, I think, onions. It was a 'special' recipe from the days when Alis was a caterer. It might have been beef stroganoff, but for us, it was simply mystery meat.

Mom and Alis were in the midst of going over the guest list to ensure there would be enough to go around. J. Dyanne was busy counting and determining how many cookies to bake.

"Okay," she began, "if we have 25 guests arriving at 6:00pm and remaining until 10:00pm, eating approximately 1 cookie every 20 minutes--"

"Just make a whole bunch of cookies," I interrupted. Great Aunt Alis looked shrewdly at J. Dyanne.

"Still blocked, huh?"

"I'm fine," she insisted. "I got all E's on my report card."

I looked with renewed hope at Alis. It was possible she could convince J. Dyanne not to trust Patrice's tale. But when I explained what happened at Grand Anne's, Alis simply shrugged. "If Anne didn't say anything, then it's okay with me."

*Mater familias* didn't raise her eyes from the task of pinching the edges of crust on the sweet potato pie.

"Don't even look at me. That's your sister's business. Besides, you've got the necklace. Just don't lose it."

This was startling. I didn't think anyone had noticed the pendant. This was my second hint that it wasn't just a trinket Grand Anne thought I'd like.

J. Dyanne was busy gathering the ingredients for her cookies. She could have been the only occupant in the kitchen for all the attention she paid to the conversation.

Since no one seemed overly concerned, I tucked the pendant away and focused on crushing graham crackers.

Thursday morning dawned bright. We'd had an overnight frost, which made the silver-tipped grass sparkle. Although I had wakened early I was not before *mater familias*. The smell of roasting turkey had filtered up to the room I shared with J. Dyanne.

The faithful hound, Dog, was sleeping next to J. Dyanne's bed. He had been keeping close these past few weeks, which was unusual. Dog was an adventurer, who wandered the streets at will. We suspected he traversed a wide area of the city. He would be gone for hours and then return with telltale signs of his journeys. Sticker bugs from the overgrown vacant lot, sand from the Johnson kid's sandbox four blocks away.

But even he seemed to sense that J. Dyanne required extra protection these days. She was resting peacefully and so I did not disturb her, but went downstairs for breakfast.

This was a simple affair on such a day as this – a bowl of hot Malt o'Meal and toast, and then the task of snapping a big bowl of string beans. I was really looking forward to tonight's feast.

The Teen Elder Others had passed through and breakfasted before J. Dyanne showed up. I had made the mistake of trying to enlist the support of the Male Teen Elder in accompanying us to the shelter that afternoon. A mistake since he had not yet finished his Rice Krispies. It was a seemingly juvenile choice for an elder teen brother, but it was serious. He never spoke until after the third serving. His answer was, simply, no. He left the table and retreated to his basement lair to shoot pool and play Jimi Hendrix records.

The Female Teen Elder didn't stop long enough

to even engage in conversation. She was in love again, which apparently meant she couldn't be outside her room for more than five minutes at a time. She confirmed that the lemon meringue pie had been made, silently prepared toast which inevitably burnt and which she insisted she liked that way, juice and back to her room to repeated rounds of listening to Jose Feliciano singing "Light My Fire."

When J. Dyanne did arrive, she seemed surprisingly upbeat, considering the family onslaught slated for the day. She went straight to the newspaper crossword once seated with her CoCo Wheats and actually invited assistance with some of the clues.

This only compounded my concerns. However, for some reason, as the time drew near for our departure, I became more optimistic about the afternoon's sojourn to the Auburn Park Shelter and Food Center. It felt as if there would be some support coming our way. This holiday was mainly filled with Watkins relatives. I ran through the short list of cousins for assistance. But Marcus and Victor would both be in basketball tournaments that afternoon and I really couldn't expect support from Darla and Darlene.

But my feelings were more than optimism. I was convinced that someone would arrive to support me in keeping J. Dyanne safe. And when there was a knock on the side door I was absolutely certain that someone had arrived.

Eagerly I opened the door to... Derek Fremont.

What was odd wasn't the fact that he was standing there holding what looked like a homemade, three-layer chocolate cake. The odd thing was that I actually felt, well, relieved to see him. It was clear he was the one I'd been waiting for. At least as far as this case was concerned.

"Derek! Just the person--" Noticing the surprise on his face, I quickly pulled myself together. "Well, what do you want?"

He gave me a strange look, then held out the cake.

"My mom... for your mom," he stuttered.

I could see he was still a bit skittish being around us after last Halloween. I tried to be cordial.

"Might as well come in." I held open the door. He was barely inside before I began explaining what was going on.

"Help Patrice Kirkwood?" he asked, his eyes suddenly alert.

"Yeah, go figure. But it's Dyanne--" I was interrupted.

"Sure. I'll go. Patrice is *fine*."

I heaved a heavy sigh. This was going to be a trial. I wanted to say never mind, but something in the back of my brain was insisting he was needed.

"Look, Derek, this is not about ogling Patrice. There are more important things--" He cut me off.

"Yeah, of course. Feeding the people." He did a Black Power salute. It was becoming a nervous habit. "Power to the people," he chanted. "I'm gonna join the Panthers. Help the community.

Soon as I graduate 8th grade."

If he was serious, that might be a good thing. I sat him down and gave him the gist of my concerns. When J. Dyanne came downstairs I expected her to be surprised. Instead, she took it in stride, as if she knew.

"Hey, Derek. You ready?"

"How did you know he was coming? Are your talents back?"

"Who needs talents when it's ridiculously obvious."

"What's obvious?" I insisted.

"Really, Katrin. Clearly you've engaged Derek's help because instead of bickering at each other from across the room you're as thick as thieves on the couch. Obvious."

We were in rather close proximity. I hastily moved away.

"It never hurts to have extra help," I suggested.

"Fine. It's a simple case though. Just don't go complicating things."

I was ready to protest, but J. Dyanne had already gathered her canvas camera bag and was headed to the door.

# Chapter 21 - The Sting

The Auburn Park Shelter and Food Center was a project in development. At present it was primarily a food center that provided free meals to those in need. The proposed residential shelter was the adjoining three-story building to the east of the food center. It was being re-modeled to accommodate its future use and was still under construction; wooden scaffolding marched up the façade; a chain-link security fence fronted the building. Heavy plastic was loosely attached to open doorways and windows, which billowed and flapped in the cold wind. The main operations were next door in the storefront.

Patrice greeted us on our arrival, twitchy and agitated. Her hair was tied back with a bandana. She wore an apron, plastic gloves and carried a wooden spoon. Not the glamorous image to which she aspired. Derek was tongue-tied.

"Hey, huh... Patrice. Yeah, hi. I'm... my name is Derek. Pleased to--"

Patrice put him out of his misery.

"What's he doing here?" she demanded. "You're going to ruin everything. I knew I shouldn't have...

oh never mind. Just, oh come on." And she turned toward the back kitchen. I turned to J. Dyanne.

"Patrice seems more on edge than usual, don't you think?"

"Good observation, Katrin. You're right." She looked thoughtfully at the retreating teen. "Maybe she's getting cold feet."

We started to follow Patrice, but were waylaid by a plumpish man in his late twenties. He wore less than attractive glasses that made him look like a black version of the Poindexter guy from the cartoons. His face held a practiced look of concern. It was that all too familiar grown-up look they thought expressed kindliness to little people, but really was pretty annoying.

"Welcome, welcome. You must be Patrice's friends come to help," he exclaimed. His voice was oddly devoid of any real feeling, though deep and clear. I wasn't getting good vibes from him at all. I looked to J. Dyanne, who was studying the serving layout. Derek simply stared at Patrice.

"Patrice, come and introduce me," the man commanded. Meekly, she came forward.

"This is Chester... Mr. Chester Morton. He's the assistant manager."

"Yes, I run the day-to-day operations here for our people. We'll keep you busy today. The unfortunate truth is that we'll have quite a crowd with us today."

"How many makes up a crowd?" J. Dyanne asked, with a quizzical look.

"Oh, well over 150 I expect. It's Thanksgiving

after all. No one likes to be alone."

J. Dyanne looked at the volunteers bringing in hotel pans filled with soup, vegetables and sliced turkey. "This isn't all, is it?" she asked.

Patrice was growing impatient. "What's it to you? This is plenty."

"Not if Mr. Morton's numbers are accurate," J. Dyanne retorted. I groaned. We were here to expose probable criminal activity and J. Dyanne was about to get mathematical about soup.

"It's quite simple. Those appear to be 20-quart trays. At one cup per serving, and four cups to a quart, that only gives you 80 servings for an estimated crowd of 150. You'll need to double the quantity or you'll run short."

Like the rest of us, Mr. Morton simply stared at Dyanne. Then he looked at Patrice as if to say, 'Who is this girl?' She simply shrugged. Morton turned his attention back to J. Dyanne.

"Well it's nothing for you to worry about." I could hear the unsaid 'little girl' in his tone. I didn't like it.

"If we run short," he continued, although clearly not convinced, "we'll just cook some more. But I'm pretty sure it'll be fine."

I remembered Grand Anne's words that something wasn't quite kosher here. I was beginning to think it was Mr. Morton.

"Patrice, give your friends a tour before we open. I'm sure they'll be interested."

We were shepherded to the back stairs. We dropped our coats and backpacks in a hall closet and followed Patrice up to the second floor.

The first stop was the business office. It was a small space crowded with two desks, chairs and file cabinets. It was sparkling clean and neat as a pin. You could still smell the cleaning chemicals.

"Is this where everything is stored?" J. Dyanne queried.

"The money and stuff, yeah. I told you it was dinky. Anyone could break in those cabinets. Go ahead, try it."

Derek immediately went forward to the filing cabinet. Apparently, he was prepared to do whatever Patrice asked of him. The drawer was locked. He jiggled the handle, but breaking and entering was obviously not his forte.

"A couple of paper clips would do it," J. Dyanne deduced. "These are, as you say, pretty dinky." She looked at Patrice's expectant look. "And no, Patrice, I'll pass." J. Dyanne looked curiously around the office. "Why not put the money in the safe?"

"The safe?" Patrice seemed momentarily confused. J. Dyanne crossed to the wall and moved aside a rather hideous picture of a sad-eyed clown, exposing a tidy little safe. Patrice seemed a bit unnerved.

"Oh, that... that hasn't worked for a while. That's why I'm worried. Until the safe gets fixed, this is where Ches... Mr. Morton is storing stuff and it's not, well, safe, you know?" Her twitchy gaze watched as J. Dyanne wandered over to the window.

"No bars on the windows and easy access to the

fire escape. This is almost too easy," she murmured.

"That's exactly what I said. But Mr. Morton thinks everybody's so honest and who would rip off a homeless shelter anyway, but I know these guys and I'm not going to be so naïve."

Well, if anything was certain, Patrice was not naïve. Not too bright, but far from innocent.

Derek was fooling around with all the desktop gadgets, getting especially excited about a handheld tape recorder.

"Whoa! This is cool. Like 007! Compact, long-playing, voice-activated. You can hide it in your pocket and no one--"

"Don't touch that!" Patrice screamed. "It's brand new!" Derek stood frozen at the outburst from his beloved. Before Patrice could snatch it, J. Dyanne calmly removed the device from Derek's clenched hands.

"It's Thanksgiving Day, Derek. Maybe by Christmas you'll convince your mom to get you one." She returned the recorder to its place on the desk, then pointed to the wall clock. "Patrice, shouldn't we get downstairs? Look at the time."

"Jeez, it's almost four. We open in ten minutes. Come on."

We headed back downstairs to prepare for the opening. At the bottom of the stairs, two men were hanging their jackets in the closet. Patrice paused as they moved on to the kitchen. She made no effort to conceal her distaste. They looked us over but said nothing.

"That's them," she whispered. "The thieves. Did you notice how rude they were? Didn't even say hello."

She proceeded to the kitchen leaving us to follow. J. Dyanne held back a moment.

"Katrin, quick... your first impression of those two men," she insisted.

"Nothing. Nothing bad anyway. In fact, I thought they seemed kinda nice, but one look at Patrice and they closed up."

"Right. Okay, Derek, did you notice the fuse box in the closet?"

"Yeah. What about it?"

"We'll need a diversion later on. I'll give you a signal, and you shut down the lights. Katrin, keep those two guys in sight. If they go missing, you let me know."

"But Dyanne, I don't think they're the--"

"Just keep them in sight, Katrin."

At that moment Morton called all the volunteers together. A long line of humanity had materialized outside the windows.

"Folks, I want to thank you all for taking time out on your Thanksgiving holiday to support our fellow brethren in need. Your smiles and good wishes will surely brighten their days." He beamed at the assembled volunteers as if he had a big treat coming their way. He paused for maximum effect.

"Today is special. Recognition is finally coming to Auburn Park," he paused, attempting to build anticipation. "You will be pleased to know... Teri

Brinker from Channel 3 News will be here, today, within minutes to share with the great city of Chicago your great contribution today."

He looked around expectantly. He wasn't disappointed. Patrice led the applause. Chester Morton was pleased. I didn't feel quite right.

"Come along now, let's line up and pray," Morton ordered.

J. Dyanne positioned herself at the end of the serving line closest to the stairs. Derek and I ranged alongside. After an interminable soliloquy, Morton finished and the doors opened.

Teri Brinker and her news team had arrived and were being escorted through the facility with a lot of pomp and circumstance by Morton and Patrice.

It was a surprise for me to see such a diverse group of people stream by. I'd only seen older homeless men and bag ladies in the news or on the streets downtown. But here were whole families, even some kids my age. They looked cold. I couldn't help but think of 7541 Winthrop and the warmth of the kitchen with *mater familias* cooking up a feast. It would be too wrong if someone did steal from this place.

As the afternoon advanced, I was just wondering if I could get some of Mom's pies over here in time, when I noticed that J. Dyanne's prediction of running short was about to be realized. The scoop I used was beginning to scrape the bottom of the pan. Patrice had already sent Derek up to the storage attic to fetch down two huge cans of government peanut butter. The dinner rolls J. Dyanne had been serving were gone. She had been in the kitchen for some time. I could bet she was calculating just how many cups of flour per biscuit were needed to feed the masses.

She returned with a basket of sliced white bread. There was a sense of heightened energy about her.

"Where are they?" she asked. I knew who she meant. I indicated the suspected thieves near the entry, guiding people through the line, keeping it orderly and friendly. Morton was in the back. Patrice was with Teri Brinker interviewing an elderly couple.

"Something's not quite right," J. Dyanne mused. I had not seen her so agitated before. Almost as twitchy as Patrice.

"Yeah, that's for sure. We're almost out of food. Not exactly the news story Morton anticipated," I said.

"Be ready," she hissed. "It's about to go down." And no sooner said than done.

There was a deep roar, and Chester Morton came storming into the main serving room.

"We've been robbed!" he shouted. "Close the doors. Nobody in! Nobody out!"

I was stunned. The two suspects had been in plain sight the entire afternoon. Morton rushed to the front door, ensured it was locked. He turned to the assembled crowd, a stern, somewhat sad expression enveloping his countenance. I didn't buy it for a minute. But Brinker and her news team were eating it up.

And, which was not at all surprising, Patrice

came screaming onto the scene. What was surprising was she had ahold of J. Dyanne's camera bag.

"It was her!" She pointed an accusing finger at J. Dyanne, with dramatic flair. "I can't believe you'd do this!"

Then in one sweeping gesture, Patrice unzipped the camera bag and grabbed a handful of cash from the inner pocket. I was stunned. I knew she was twisted, but I didn't expect this.

Before I could find a suitable response, the entire scene went black and my arm was nearly jerked out of its socket.

# Chapter 22 - Gimme Shelter

Stumbling in the dark upstairs, while pandemonium reigned down below, I was still reeling from Patrice's betrayal. Derek was mumbling what might have been curses, but I couldn't make them out. J. Dyanne was silent as we raced up more stairs, dimly lit by emergency lighting. We bypassed the second floor, heading to the attic. It seemed she had a plan.

We reached the top floor, which had an open floor plan, though stacked with supplies, crates and tables. The streetlights shone through the bare windows, giving us just enough of an advantage to make our way to the windows.

"Okay, listen, we've got to make it down before they figure out about the lights. Quick work, Derek."

We tried the windows, but they were stuck. On closer inspection, we could see they were painted shut. It was colder up here, and the reason was clear. The west wall had been knocked out to create an opening to the next building. It was covered with plastic sheeting but you could still feel a definite breeze. Without jackets, Chicago's autumn air was fierce against our skin. But escape was paramount. We had no choice but to go through the wall.

Derek ripped down a corner of the heavy plastic, creating an entry. The blast of cold intensified. I was nearly through to the other building when I turned to see J. Dyanne standing, transfixed by the windows.

"Dyanne, hurry, they're coming."

And indeed the echoes of footsteps were getting louder. J. Dyanne shook herself free of whatever had stalled her movement and came forward. Stepping into the construction site, she paused again, as did we all. Weak light filtered through the translucent plastic on the windows on the street side. But the window by the fire escape was boarded up. We would have to get downstairs and find an exit.

"This is the place," J. Dyanne muttered.

"Yeah, it's the place where we'll get caught if we don't hurry," Derek retorted. "Come on."

Moving toward what we hoped were stairs, I could hear the crackle of freezing rain on plastic sheets. Looking up, a domed skylight was leaking rain. Unfinished walls stood with exposed two-by-four beams standing in straight lines like skeletal soldiers. Workbenches were shrouded in drop cloths, giving the illusion of huddled specters. It was cold, damp and dark. At least the floor was solid. The rickety stairs strained under our weight but held, more or less. Derek put a foot through one of the treads, but we made it to the second floor intact. It was darker here, without the benefit of the skylight. Out of the corner of my eye, I saw a wisp of light. Turning round, I saw J. Dyanne. She was tracking something, turning slowly in a complete circle, then standing still.

"What?" she asked the empty space. Derek and I watched with some misgiving as she continued the conversation. We could hear the commotion next door and knew time was of the essence.

"Sorry. Okay, I'll listen... Tangled web... okay, thanks. I owe you." She turned her attention to us. "What're you staring at? Let's move." And she headed down the next flight of stairs.

I turned to follow, when I heard what sounded like a piteous wail, followed by a deafening crash. It stopped me in my tracks.

"Oh, hell," muttered Derek. He grabbed my arm and pulled me toward the stairs.

"Don't worry," J. Dyanne said. "That's just a friend causing a little diversion." Yeah, well there are friends and then there are J. Dyanne's friends.

We got to the entry and pushed through the plastic into the rain.

Despite the inclement weather, the front of the food center was crowded with the people locked out when Morton shut the place down. Police sirens shattered the late afternoon dark. We huddled in the shadow of the scaffolding, unseen by the crowd. I wanted to ask about J. Dyanne's one-sided conversation, but my teeth had begun to chatter from the cold.

"Okay, Jacqueléne, what do we do next?" demanded Derek. J. Dyanne looked toward the food center entrance. There was some urgency, as the sirens were drawing closer. For some reason, the only thought in my mind was Grand Anne. It seemed J. Dyanne had the same idea.

"We can find shelter at Yemaya. Grand Anne won't mind a little breaking and entering," she said.

"No need. She's already there," I said with a confidence that surprised even me. J. Dyanne gave me an odd look, then grabbed hold of the chain link fence and climbed over. There was a loud clatter as she temporarily lost her footing and dislodged the construction company sign. Derek and I quickly followed. We found J. Dyanne squinting down at the sign. Derek moved to replace it, but she held him back.

"Leave it," she said. "R&R Brothers have more to worry about than a broken sign. Let's get going."

No one needed any more prompting. We covered the three blocks in record time. And sure enough, we could see a soft light glowing through the front window as we turned the last corner. Grand Anne let us in without question or surprise and led us to the back, turning off the front lights.

The first sensation that hit was the warmth and smell of apple spice tea. The next was the chatter from the television. It was clearly Channel 3 News. Patrice's fake, tear-stained face was dead center, live from the Auburn Park Shelter and Food Center. In the background of the shot was the open office where police had begun their investigation. Derek lost his cool.

"She's evil. Just plain evil. Turn it off. I never want to see her--" Grand Anne stopped him.

"Well, Jacqueléne? Which talent will get you out of this one?" I couldn't stand it. I had to come to J. Dyanne's defense.

"Grand Anne, it's not Dyanne's fault. Who could possibly know what Patrice was planning?"

"You knew. Or at least you knew better than to trust her," Grand Anne countered. "You even made sure you had support on this little adventure."

She indicated Derek.

"You'll come into your own soon, Katrin." She then touched the pendant I still wore. "This particular stone is called Labradorite. It enhanced your latent intuition, which was useful." She turned again to J. Dyanne.

"But right now, Jacqueléne needs to decide what she's going to do."

We all turned to her. She was watching the TV screen.

"Right now? Well, right now, I can only hope that what I know about Patrice's mind holds true." She turned to Grand Anne. "I'll need to use your phone."

Grand Anne nodded. J. Dyanne took a business card from her jeans pocket, picked up the receiver and dialed.

On the television screen, the chatter stopped, as everyone turned to the ringing office phone.

# Chapter 23 - End Game

The camera zoomed in on the ringing phone. A white-gloved officer pressed the speakerphone feature. J. Dyanne's voice came on in stereo.

"This is Jacqueléne Dyanne DuBois, the falsely accused thief." The cameraman pulled out to capture the stunned faces of everyone in the office, as well as those standing outside in the hall. Patrice looked nervous. Chester Morton stood like a statue, his face devoid of emotion. The officer spoke.

"Your parents have been notified, young lady. It will be best if you and your friends come in and explain yourselves."

"Before we come in Officer, there is something you should know." I had no idea how J. Dyanne was going to talk herself out of this one. It was her word against Patrice and Chester Morton. But as I've said before, J. Dyanne was no dummy.

"Located on the desk in front of you is a recording device. You'll note that it is a new model that has a voice-activated feature. I would ask that you rewind and play the tape." Patrice's familiar piercing scream could be heard.

"It's a lie. Whatever she says is a lie!" Patrice

tried to rush the desk, but was restrained by the officer at the door. This was becoming a bit of a habit with her.

"Sorry miss. This is a crime scene. You cannot enter."

Meantime, the first officer had rewound the tape. He pressed "play." Once again, J. Dyanne's voice was heard.

*"It's Thanksgiving Day, Derek. Maybe by Christmas you'll convince your mom to get you one."* A pause, and then: *"Patrice, shouldn't we get downstairs? Look at the time."*

*"Jeez, it's almost four. We open in ten minutes. Come on."*

Patrice tried to leave the scene, but was again held up by the officer. There was silence and then the tape picked up again. Patrice's voice filled the room.

*"Put on your gloves. Fingerprints, remember? Over here. That kid tried to open the top drawer."*

I heard J. Dyanne breathe a sigh of relief. She had guessed right. There was a pause in the recording and then the sound of scraping metal. One look at the mangled file drawer in the background and it was clear that it had been wrenched open.

*"Hurry! They're running out of food, and trash news Teri's getting bored,"* Patrice continued. That remark was going to cost Patrice big-time. You don't mess with the media.

A new voice was heard, and wasn't it a surprise. Assistant Manager Chester Morton.

*"They won't leave once we give them this story.*

*I can hear Teri Brinker now,"* His voice took on a high-pitched tone. *"'Live from Auburn Park Shelter and Food Center. Hundreds left hungry after Thanksgiving Day robbery!'"*

*"We can laugh about that in the Bahamas. Right now, I'll need to put some of the money in her bag,"* came the ever-practical voice of Patrice.

*"Not too much. Just use singles. We'll put the rest in the safe."* Patrice's evil laugh was heard.

*"Don't worry, Chester. There'll be plenty left for us."* The tape went silent on the echoes of their laughter.

A third officer took Chester Morton by the arm. He looked stonily at the camera. "I wish to speak with my attorney."

The camera then switched back to the phone in the office where J. Dyanne's voice was coming through.

"Thank you for listening, Officer. We'll be happy to come down there now." Before she could hang up, Teri Brinker called out across the room.

"Miss DuBois, this is Channel 3 News journalist Teri Brinker. Now that you've cleared your name, do you have a message for the true, bumbling, idiot thieves on this Thanksgiving Day?

"Uh, no...," she began. Then she perked up.

"But I do have a message for your viewers, Miss Brinker. There are close to 80 people down here who still don't have a Thanksgiving meal. If 25 households set aside 3.2 plates of food and brought them over here, then everyone would be fed. And don't forget dessert!" J. Dyanne grinned over at me.

I grinned back. I suppose some math problems aren't so bad.

* * *

As predicted, Channel 3's Teri Brinker had a field day with the story. She showed Patrice Kirkwood no mercy. Brinker had gone to the archives and pulled up the story from last August. She put the blame fully on Patrice for enticing the preacher's kid into the kidnapping plot just as she had persuaded the deluded Chester Morton she was in love with him. Patrice would be forever branded as something of a teen bad seed that all sensible men should avoid. As it turned out, this wouldn't be too difficult. One year shy of her 18th birthday, it seemed Patrice would surely be headed to a girl's detention center.

Chester Morton was fired immediately and the general manager of the shelter took over the hands-on operations, assuring patrons that everything would be moving forward in a just and righteous manner.

J. Dyanne's televised math problem generated an outpouring of support from several local neighborhoods. Even Warren showed up with a trunk load of food compliments of Alderman Weaver. And of course, *mater* and *pater familias* showed up with all of the pies, along with Grand Anne and Great Aunt Alis. Even the Teen Elder Others came with them. I suspect they weren't going to let the day go by without a slice of Mom's sweet potato or lemon meringue. It was a great Thanksgiving feast for all concerned.

* * *

During the course of the evening, J. Dyanne and I sat down with Grand Anne and Great Aunt Alis.

"Well?" said Alis. J. Dyanne squirmed a bit.

"Use it or lose it," said Grand Anne. "It's your choice."

J. Dyanne still did not respond. Grand Anne went on.

"You aren't in this alone." A soft smile crossed her face. She turned to Aunt Alis.

"Remember Mama Susie? She was a taskmaster she was." Alis nodded.

"She was that. And I thank her every day. Saved my life more than once." Alis took J. Dyanne's hand.

"Your talent has a long tradition, girly. I don't know the end, but I do know it has a purpose. You can take it to the next generation."

"And you can also let it go," Grand Anne said. "As you say, you've got other talents. And they are useful and you'll probably have a fine life."

"But?" J. Dyanne asked.

"But nothing," said Alis. "What needs to happen will happen with or without you. It'll just take a little longer, maybe." I couldn't stand it.

"What needs to happen? What are you talking about?"

Grand Anne gave a deep sigh. I recognized it as a trait often seen in J. Dyanne. It had something to do with a kind of acceptance of the inevitable.

"You have been born to a purpose. The task is to discover this purpose and bring it forward into the world. You are at the time of life where you begin your discovery."

"You make it sound like I'm some kind of 'chosen one' or something."

Alis and Grand Anne exchanged looks and smiled.

"Of course you are, Jacqueléne," Grand Anne responded.

J. Dyanne sat frozen in her chair. "You can't be serious."

"Oh yes. But the question you need to ask is: for what have you been chosen?" Alis picked up the thread.

"Despite the myths and legends we read about, there has never been just a single 'chosen one' because we are each chosen for a purpose. No person is born without one. Maybe you've been chosen to be a leader. Maybe you've been chosen to be a healer. You are the only one who can discover what you have been born to do."

"And so, again the question to you, Jacqueléne Dyanne DuBois, is: Well?"

J. Dyanne got that watchful, wistful look on her face that betokened an advanced state of concentration. I was beginning to know it well. And then she too gave a deep sigh. I knew then that she was ready to accept all of her talents, not just the logical ones but the intuitive and intangible ones as well.

Nothing more was said. Words were no longer needed. Not with this group. Even I could sense that we had moved to a new place of adventure and discovery.

I could hardly wait.

# Chapter 24 - Media Savvy

The Friday after Thanksgiving is known as the busiest shopping day in the Chicago Loop. The hub of the city, at State and Madison – where all street numbers begin – is ambushed annually by holiday shoppers. We never join in.

This year would have been impossible anyway. The premises of 7541 were jammed with people. Family, neighbors, pets. Everyone had heard of J. Dyanne's latest adventure at the shelter. And everyone wanted to talk about it. Even Teri Brinker showed up trying for an exclusive, one-on-one. This time J. Dyanne couldn't run off to the library. But Mom finally asked Brinker to leave. She did, but only retreated to the sidewalk. Nicole Trotter rushed in to tell us that some of the kids were telling big lies about J. Dyanne to Brinker.

"I told that news lady not to listen to them calling you a witch. George McIntyre was talking about some teacher at your school. And Derek Fremont tried to stop his mom, but she was talking on and on about some ghost you talked to in a picture. But I told her that you were not a ghost and that you found my dog and you were powerful, like

Wonder Woman and I was your friend."

You must understand that Nicole had four older brothers who were comic book fanatics, so naturally she would reference Wonder Woman. But what she didn't realize was how she had contributed to J. Dyanne's worst nightmare – publicity.

"Thanks, Nicole. Is she still out there?" J. Dyanne asked.

"Yeah. Audrey Clayton is talking to her now."

This was of concern. Audrey was one of Patrice's best friends. That was the final straw. I followed J. Dyanne out to the front porch. It was trying to snow, but it was more like intermittent ice pellets. But it didn't stop Audrey from trying to get on television. When we came out, Teri Brinker immediately came forward to the shelter of the porch. Derek rushed up after her.

"I tried to stop them, but she wouldn't leave," he panted.

"Miss Dubois, is it true you can talk to the dead?" asked Brinker. J. Dyanne looked at the cameraman and the crowd, then back at the newswoman.

"I've got something you'll want to hear. An exclusive. But I need a promise from you. Off camera."

"That depends, Miss Dubois."

"Promise?"

Brinker considered her for a moment, then turned to the cameraman.

"Shut it off." She handed him her microphone. "This better be good."

J. Dyanne led her to the far side of the porch

away from the camera and the crowd on the sidewalk.

"Look, I really hate publicity. If you promise not to use anything these people said, I'll give you a scoop on something big."

"Like what?"

"Like political corruption, bribery?" That certainly caught Brinker's attention.

"Go on."

"What if I told you there's more to that shelter story? That it's deeper than Patrice Kirkwood and her feeble attempt at embezzlement?"

"If you had that kind of story, I can assure you I can keep these interviews off the air."

"I do have that story. It'll make a nice Christmas present for you."

"Then you've got a deal." Brinker gave her the number to the station, packed up her crew and left. Nicole looked up at her idol, just a tad worried.

"Did I do something wrong?"

"No, it's not your fault. I know you were just trying to help. Thanks."

J. Dyanne got that watchful look in her eyes.

"I've got a plan," she said, and refocused on us. "You all game?" Nicole nodded eagerly. Derek shrugged assent. Naturally, I was game. J. Dyanne beckoned us inside.

Upstairs, she pulled out the photos of Miss Reynolds at Weaver's office.

"Nicole, how often do you walk Buddy?"

"Before school and when I get home."

"Okay, see this woman? She used to work for

Alderman Weaver. Maybe still does. I want you to keep an eye on Weaver's office. You know where it is, right?"

"Yeah, next to the Ace Hardware."

"Right. Walk Buddy over that way, and report back to me if you see her or anything unusual. Got it?"

"You bet." Nicole was thrilled.

"Derek, we need to find out more about Miss Reynolds. Where she lives. Even her first name would be nice. Maybe somebody at Frieda's Corner Stop might know something about her. Or the donut shop across the street. Okay?" Derek nodded.

"Katrin and I start helping out at Yemaya tomorrow. We'll also stop by the shelter. There're a couple things I need to see in daylight. Derek, meet us at the church tomorrow around two o'clock. Nicole, you stick to your assignment. That's all."

"Whoa, wait just a minute. You haven't told us about what happened yesterday with you talking to the air. You gotta admit, Jackalini, that was pretty weird."

"You the one who's weird, Derek Fremont," shouted Nicole.

"Easy... easy." J. Dyanne gave a resigned sigh. "I guess it looked weird." She turned to Nicole. "Don't freak out. It's just a little something that happens to me sometimes."

"One of the ancestors?" I ventured.

"Not exactly. It was Emmitt. He used to live there."

"Used to?"

"Yeah, that building has a lot of spirit vibes."

"I knew it! You have been dreaming," I asserted.

"Of course. Emmitt's been trying to reach me since I visited there with Weaver last month. But I was ignoring him. He wasn't too pleased. But after I apologized, he told me to remember about the tangled web and he would distract the posse so we could escape." Nicole was nearly speechless.

"You can talk to spirits? You're better than Wonder Woman."

"'*Oh what a tangled web we weave when first we practice to deceive.*'" I murmured.

"That's Shakespeare," said Derek.

"No. Sir Walter Scott," I said.

"Shakespeare," he insisted.

"Look it up later," J. Dyanne interrupted. "Anyway, like I told Brinker, there's more to this than Patrice being mad at me. We've got ourselves a weaver and it's time to untangle his web of deception. So you all be careful."

In my mind, J. Dyanne was the one who needed to be careful.

## Chapter 25 - Travelers

"There is one universal vibration. One energy. There are those who recognize this and are able to work, communicate and live within the flow of the natural universe. Through the years, this link has had many names. Some call it psychic, others a gift, and still others call it a curse. I know it as a talent."

Our lessons with Grand Anne had begun. We were seated in the back room at Yemaya. It was warm with the varied scents of fragrant oils and herbs. The Wisdom Reading cloth was laid out on the table. J. Dyanne and I sat listening to Grand Anne while we sipped spiced apple tea and munched on chocolate chip cookies.

"As you know, everyone has talent to some degree," Grand Anne continued. "It is as fluid as your breath, as personal as your own voice. Yet it is elusive, glimpsed by some, while others are firm in their denial that such talent even exists. Only a few are awake to the full awareness of its presence."

As she spoke, Grand Anne placed a Wisdom Card on the reading cloth. First was the Affinity card, depicting a vast ocean, the half circle of the rising sun artfully inverted in the shimmering water at the horizon to form a perfect orb. The symbols of the four goals: the spiral, bowl of fire, coin and temple dome encircled the sun. She turned to J. Dyanne.

"Without thinking about it, you've accessed your talent. You have a sensitivity that allows you to see through the different layers of people, time and space. And you have the logical mind of a mathematician – a dynamite combination. You'll want to examine what this means."

Next she placed the card for Discovery. This showed a young girl of the Victorian era. Her blonde hair flowed to her shoulders from a topknot, and featherlike bangs fluttered on her forehead. She was in a smoky laboratory, test tubes in hand and elaborate glass beakers of liquid simmered over dancing flames.

"This path is yours to discover. You're a Traveler – just at the cusp of what could be a long journey."

"Could be?" J. Dyanne asked.

"Yes. You are of age to choose. Remember that – you always have a choice."

She now placed the card for The Traveler on the cloth – this was a shadowy design of a railroad platform, the Traveler in silhouette, the destination unclear.

"On the path of the Traveler," Grand Anne went on, "you will attract both positive and negative energy. You can learn from both. And there are those who will challenge you in the hope of negating your talent, of silencing your voice. Many choose not to travel this road."

"And if I don't choose?"

"You tell me. What was it like last month?"

"Okay, okay," J. Dyanne laughed. "I choose. I have chosen."

"So now, you need your tools." Grand Anne reached for a brand new composition book. She handed it to me, with a sleek new Paper Mate pen.

"Your task is to keep a record." I didn't mind. My most favorite book in the world is a blank composition book – all fresh and ready to fill up with adventures and wonder. Grand Anne then gathered up the Wisdom Cards and sorted through them.

"Do you have any questions from your studies?" she asked.

"Alderman Weaver said something about him being related to me." J. Dyanne ventured. "Is he a Traveler?"

"James Everett Weaver. Actually, he is a Relative; one who accepts his talents, but doesn't work to develop them further."

"But he uses them," I interjected. "He tried to use them on Dyanne. I saw it."

Grand Anne and J. Dyanne looked at me in surprise.

"You 'saw' it?" Grand Anne asked. She looked intrigued. "Was this before or after I gave you the pendant?"

"Hmmm, before. Why?"

"Never mind that. Tell me, what did you see?"

"Well, his eyes were sort of glassy and then I could see, you know, like when it's really hot and you kind of see heat waves? Well, it was like that. Only it was like a breeze... a cool, wavy breeze."

"Did you try to interact with what you saw? Try to block it?" Grand Anne asked.

"No. It was fast and it just passed right over Dyanne. Didn't affect her at all, so I didn't really think about it much."

"Okay, well it looks like we have more work to do than I thought." She put away the cards, except for one.

"What are the four goals?"

"Duty, Well-Being, Abundance and Affinity," we recited.

"The first goal is Duty. And to fulfill your duty, you need a foundation of Discipline." Grand Anne placed the Discipline card in the center of the table.

The image here showed another young girl of the Victorian Era, only she looked a lot like J. Dyanne, square-jawed and brown-skinned, her hair and clothes blown by a whirlwind. The surrounding landscape was windswept as well – trees bent, leaves swirling overhead. The girl was balanced on a downed tree trunk that formed a bridge across a turbulent river. Though her surroundings were swirling, the girl stood straight and confident. In her hand she carried a candle. Despite the tumult around her, the candle flame was steady and bright.

"The Discipline to master is to be still. Not simply in your seats, like they tell you at school. But inside. You must learn to access the still space within you, because this is where the heart of your talent lives."

That morning we learned how to breathe in a way that calmed down all the muscles and even the organs of the body. Sometimes it didn't even feel like we were breathing at all; it was so smooth it didn't register as breathing.

"Katrin, I'm going to access my own talent," Grand Anne said. "Tell me if you can sense it."

Like the first time Weaver tried to read me, I did feel a wave of energy seep into my mind. I pushed back.

"No, Katrin, not outward. Stay with your own stillness. Let your energy block it, not your mind." I made the adjustment. And I could see the energy waves shift away like bouncing off an invisible shield.

"Ah, very good." She turned to J. Dyanne.

"Now, let's work with you. What you need to remember is that you don't want to ignore spirit communication. They just get more persistent and irritating."

"Tell me about it."

"Oh, so you tried it? Then you know what I'm talking about. What you want to do is to tell them, in no uncertain terms, when, where and to what extent you are willing to be available."

"That'll work?"

"Usually. You've got Katrin to support you. And

your parents. They're both Relatives in more ways than blood. Just as you two are bonded by more than sisterhood. Don't let anybody divide you from each other. Remember that and you'll be fine."

We left Grand Anne to her customers and walked through the icy snow-rain to the shelter. There was no work going on at the construction site, but J. Dyanne looked around anyway. She took a closer look at the sign knocked down the day before. The glue holding the sticker with the company's name had been loosened by the wet weather, so she peeled it back. The sign had originally belonged to a company called Sadowski and Sons Construction.

"What are you doing? Stop!"

We looked up to find Miss Reynolds glaring at us. Once she recognized who we were, her expression changed.

"Why are you here?" she snapped. "Leave that sign alone. Haven't you done enough damage?"

"But what are you... I mean do you live around here?"

"I work here now since you got me fired." She saw we looked skeptical and for reasons of her own, blurted out an explanation. "I mean, I saw what happened on TV, and knew they'd need someone, so I came to volunteer. And the general manager, well he hired me."

Miss Reynolds was not a very good liar. You can tell a lie when the person starts running off at the mouth. She seemed to realize this, snatched the sign from J. Dyanne and hung it on the gate, making a valiant effort to make the sticker stick again.

"I should have you arrested for vandalism. Just wait till my father hears about this." And on that barb, she pushed off down the street.

"What has her father got to do with anything?" I wondered.

"It's obvious, Katrin," J. Dyanne said and headed to the bus stop without explaining.

I really hate it when she does that.

* * *

Mom was already set up for us when we got to the church, and Derek was early. As church secretary Mom designed and typed up the Sunday service programs each week. We were often enlisted to help collate, fold and staple the finished product. The pages were stacked in an assembly-line fashion. We would walk the line, stack a program, staple it in the middle, fold and stack again. Derek gave us his update when Mom went to make more copies.

"Everybody seems to know Miss Reynolds. First name is Dolores. She lives on South Parkw... I mean, the Reverend Dr. Martin Luther King, Jr. Drive." Chicago was the first city to re-name a street for Dr. King, and like Derek, most of us used his full name. It was like music.

"According to Carl over at Frieda's, she wasn't the most friendly person. Thought she was made for better things, like moving up to the alderman's downtown office at City Hall. Didn't want any part of the family's construction business... Hey! R&R

Bros.! That was on the sign. You think it's Reynolds and Reynolds?"

"We saw her over at the shelter," I interjected. "She works there now."

"That's fast."

"Smooth is what I call it," J. Dyanne added. "How does she go from getting fired for stealing petty cash, to managing a food center?"

"And right next door to the family's construction site," Derek concluded.

"Remember when I found the discrepancy in the petty cash?" J. Dyanne continued. "Weaver was ready to overlook it. But since you were writing about it and there were witnesses he had to act. So, he fired Miss Reynolds."

"Why would he overlook somebody taking his cash?" Derek asked.

"Maybe because it wasn't her," J. Dyanne went on. "I mean, let's face it. Does Dolores Reynolds seem like the type who could embezzle from someone like Weaver without him knowing about it? His talent allows him to sense people's motivations."

"So maybe they were in it together and she was upset because he was forcing her to take the fall."

"Right. And he had to make up for it," Derek surmised. "So, Weaver promised to get her something else. And he came through in spades. Not only does Reynolds get to manage the shelter, her father and brothers get the contract on re-building the shelter."

"Wonder what other money scams he's pulling,"

J. Dyanne said.

"You'll need proof if you go around spouting such serious accusations, young lady."

We were so busy collating and talking we hadn't heard Rev. Ingle enter the office.

"We'll get it," J. Dyanne asserted.

"Uh-huh. Well, you just keep in mind that this here is Chicago and you're dealing with a politician."

"We'll definitely keep that in mind," I affirmed. Rev. Ingle chuckled.

"I told Weaver he better be careful having you girls around."

He turned toward the door, and then hesitated.

"I guess I owe you a favor after how you helped me last summer. So, if you find yourself in a pickle, well, you know where to find me." And he left. We were still standing around staring at each other when Mom returned with more programs.

"What're you all doing standing there like bumps on a log? We've got work to do."

As the old folks say, 'Truer words were never spoke.'

## Chapter 26 - The Link Boy

December 1968

There were only two weeks before Christmas break and we had a lot of ground to cover. Sunday was Dad's birthday. We gave him his annual gift of Old Spice cologne and while we devoured one of Mom's homemade 1-2-3 cakes, we also pumped Dad for information about construction companies. This was his field of expertise after all.

"Sadowski and Sons? Yeah, I know 'em. They get a lot of contracts out this way. Based out of South Chicago. Do good work. Why?"

"They used to have the contract on the shelter, but the new contractors are R&R Brothers."

"Frank and Richard Reynolds. They pulled Sadowski off and put on Reynolds?"

"Looks that way. Is that odd?"

"Don't know about odd. Sadowski? He's got a solid track record. Reynolds? Pretty new in the field."

Dad slowly finished off his second slice of cake. Then leaned back with his coffee. You don't rush Dad. Not if you want an answer. He finally looked at J. Dyanne.

"What's your game?"

J. Dyanne explained her theory about Alderman Weaver. Dad heard her out in silence, then poured himself more coffee, shaking his head in a bemused kind of way.

"What?" J. Dyanne asked. "You don't think I'm right?"

"Not at all. I don't doubt you. I just never thought you were interested in politics."

"I'm not," J. Dyanne insisted. "But if I see something's not right, shouldn't I try and do something about it?"

"Yes. Just keep in mind who you're dealing with. Weaver's not some schoolyard bully you want sent to the principal's office, understand?"

We both nodded.

"So, I got two things to say. One, don't make a move against this man without checking with me. And two, I think we need to find out who owns that building."

It was a relief to have Dad on the team. With his construction contacts, all he had to do was make a couple of phone calls to find out a key piece to the puzzle. James Everett Weaver was the owner of both the food center and the shelter next door. We now had a tangible connection with him, Miss Reynolds and the construction site.

J. Dyanne set up a strategy board using one of the poster boards from her science project. She placed all the known Weaver connections in red. Derek and Nicole came over to report on their findings. Nicole hadn't seen the woman, but there was a white man who came to the office. In a truck.

"When he left, his face was all red. I think he was mad. You know how Mr. Pinsky, the track coach, looks when he gets mad? His face goes all funny colored. This man didn't look like that when he went in, but he did when he came out."

"Was there any writing on the truck?"

"Yeah, but I can't pronounce it. One of those 'ski' names, you know?"

"Sadowski?" I prompted.

"Yeah, that could be it. It started with a 'S' too."

I wrote it on the board and Nicole confirmed it.

"We need to get in Weaver's office and take another look at the books."

"You mean break in or something?"

"No, we can do better than that," J. Dyanne said. "Weaver goes to his downtown office on Monday. We'll just make a visit to Mrs. Walker."

It was times like these that made me glad to have the labradorite pendant. Grand Anne said that it enhanced my intuition, which would definitely be useful going into an undercover operation like this. So far I wasn't getting any negative vibes. So, we proceeded with the plan.

When we got off the bus the next day, Derek, Nicole and Buddy were waiting for us at the bus stop.

"No sign of Weaver or his driver. Figure they must be down at City Hall. The receptionist is there by herself," Derek reported.

"Good. Stick to the plan. Nicole, you and Buddy are on lookout, in case Weaver shows up. Derek--"

"I will be the charming distraction to Mrs. Walker, while you scope out Weaver's office."

"Katrin, you might have to back him up on that. Okay, let's move."

Phase One was no problem. Mrs. Walker immediately buzzed us in.

"Well, good afternoon girls. What can I do for you?"

"Good afternoon, Mrs. Walker." I poured on my most innocent smile. "Is Alderman Weaver here?"

"Now, don't you remember? The Alderman is at City Hall on Monday. You want to leave him a message?"

"Well, actually," J. Dyanne piped up. "I need to follow up on my assignment." She started pulling out her camera stuff as she spoke. "See, the pictures I took for my Social Studies notebook didn't come out right. Bad film. And I need a cover photo and a picture of the Alderman's office; you know he's got that desk with the flags and everything. And the city ward map, things like that. I want to get a really good grade."

"Uh-huh. And who is this young man?" Derek stepped up to the occasion. He actually could be charming, in an awkward sort of way.

"Hi, I'm Derek Fremont."

"Oh yes, you're the brother of that sailor the Alderman saved down in Mexico. Well, you kids take care you don't break anything. I'll just let the Alderman know you stopped by..."

"No!" J. Dyanne nearly shouted. "I mean... I want to surprise the Alderman with a... copy of my Social Studies notebook."

"For Christmas!" I added. "As a thank you present."

"Well, aren't you sweet? Well, go on then. And be careful."

Phase Two was in motion. I followed J. Dyanne to the office, while Derek stayed at the reception desk engaging Mrs. Walker. I stood between the office and the reception area to make sure Mrs. Walker didn't decide to come back and see what J. Dyanne was really doing, which was going through Weaver's files and taking pictures of them. It was quick work. All those days doing the filing made everything easy to find. But I was starting to feel antsy.

"Hurry up," I whispered. "Derek's running out of small talk."

"The ledgers. They're not in the file cabinet." J. Dyanne tried the desk drawers, but they were locked. "I'm gonna have to pick 'em." She took a couple of paper clips from the desk tray and set to work. I heard Derek rambling on.

"I think you would make a great politician Mrs. Walker. Have you ever thought about running for office yourself?"

He was really piling it on thick. Though it was working smoothly, my antsy-ness went up a notch. J. Dyanne had worked the lock and found the ledgers, just as Buddy started making a racket out back. Someone was coming. I heard tires rolling over the gravel outside. J. Dyanne was clicking shots as fast as she could. A key was fitted into the door at the back of the office. And then Nicole's voice rose over Buddy's barking.

"Hey mister! You left your car running."

"I won't be long, but thanks for the heads up."

Thanks, indeed. J. Dyanne stepped into the hallway just as Warren Murphy walked in. He stopped when he saw us, his expression going from surprise to suspicion very quickly.

"What's going on here?" he snapped.

"Hi Warren! Good to see you," I said. J. Dyanne was focusing her camera on the city ward map. She casually looked over at Warren.

"Hi! Just needed a few pictures for my Social Studies notebook." She turned to me. "I'm all done. You ready?"

"Oh yeah," I breathed. "I'm ready."

Phase Three – we got out. Fast.

"That was so cool. Just like *Mission: Impossible*." Derek started humming the theme song as we hurried down the street.

"Nicole, you were Wonder Woman today."

"Thanks. And Buddy's gonna get a nice treat when we get home."

"What do we do next, Jackalini?"

"I develop the photos and find proof. Then we decide the next steps." I thought the investigation was going well. That is, until we met with Grand Anne.

# Chapter 27 - Stillness

"How many times do you need to hear this?" Grand Anne was not pleased. "First Aunt Alis told you. I told you last week. You need to remember these things on your own without me having to remind you all the time." Grand Anne stopped and took a breath. We were in the back room of Yemaya for our weekly lesson. J. Dyanne and I were both a little agitated because there were still leads to follow. We had eagerly explained our progress to Grand Anne, which had led to this outburst.

"Jacqueléne. Katrin. I'm not saying you should ignore facts or practical reality. What I'm saying is that those are only part of the picture. You have the ability to see to a deeper level in this situation. Use it. It can only help you achieve your goal. And, more important, it will keep you safe."

I realized then that Grand Anne wasn't angry. She was worried. During the past week we had been focused on our investigation, not to mention school and the resulting homework. Mr. Gordon had once again assigned a NASA Notebook for the upcoming Apollo 8 mission to orbit the moon. Gordon was really excited about this one – the first manned space flight actually entering the orbit of the moon. I was afraid to think of the assignment he'd give us if we actually landed on the moon. Hopefully, I'd be out of school by then.

The point Grand Anne was making was that we hadn't done any of the homework she'd given us. We hadn't studied the Wisdom Cards at all, and we certainly didn't practice stillness unless we were asleep.

"Now, what did you learn last week?"

"Learn to be still," J. Dyanne replied.

"Why?"

"Learn to access the still space within, because this is where the heart of your talent lives." Memorization was always my strong point.

"And did you do this? No." Grand Anne took another, deeper breath. "I suppose this is new for you. But it is important that you make this a daily practice. When you connect to that energy inside yourselves, you connect to the one energy in all of us. So, do it. It should be so much a part of you it happens spontaneously." She poured more tea. Took a sip. We waited. In silence.

"You have active, inquisitive minds. That's good. You need a good mind for the work you have done and will do. And... the mind also needs time to rest. To rejuvenate.

And so we became still.

It wasn't comfortable at first. There were so many thoughts, images and feelings floating around. But it settled down. Just when I thought I was getting the hang of it, I heard J. Dyanne cry out.

"Patrice!"

I opened my eyes and saw J. Dyanne had pushed away from the table and stood staring at the opposite wall. Grand Anne went to J. Dyanne and guided her back to her seat. Soon, her eyes re-focused and she sat looking down at her teacup.

"Go on. Drink. It will help." This wasn't the spice apple tea. I could smell chamomile and roses. J. Dyanne dutifully drank. Grand Anne pointed at the composition book then turned to J. Dyanne.

"Now, what about Patrice?"

"She's not in detention. Miss Reynolds was in a cage and Patrice was laughing, holding the key."

"What else?"

"Miss Reynolds was just sitting there. Crying."

"Good. Now, don't try to reason it out right now. Just let it sit. Anything else comes up, take a few notes, don't elaborate, just write exactly what comes up. Katrin can help you with that. Sleep on it. Then tomorrow, first thing, use the Wisdom Cards and see what they say."

Grand Anne started collecting the tea things. I quickly chronicled J. Dyanne's episode and Grand Anne's instructions in the composition book. It was time to open the store.

That afternoon, Derek and Nicole brought over extra newspapers and magazines. While we sorted through for articles and pictures about the Apollo mission, we discussed the case. Sure enough, Nicole confirmed about Patrice.

"I saw her. She and Audrey Clayton were over at

Frieda's Corner Stop laughing and giggling over some stupid magazines."

"Mrs. Walker said that Chester Morton was a bad influence who corrupted that 'poor child.'" Derek let out a derisive snort. "I'm pretty sure it was the other way around."

"Mrs. Walker is Derek's new girlfriend," teased Nicole.

"Hey, she's a source. I'm just using a source."

"Don't break her heart, lover-boy." It was nice to see him get taunted for a change. And Nicole was good at it.

"That's it!" J. Dyanne said. "Miss Reynolds. She was broken-hearted, that's why she was crying."

"You think she was in love with Morton?" I took out my composition book. "I mean, if Patrice was going to run off with Morton and Miss Reynolds was in love with Morton, then she'd be broken-hearted."

"Remember what Grand Anne said," J. Dyanne reminded me. "Don't reason it out. Just take notes."

"What in the world are you talking about?" demanded Derek.

We explained about today's lesson, but stopped the discussion when Derek tried to add his own hypothesis. We were going to follow Grand Anne's instructions this time.

The next morning we got out the cards. J. Dyanne laid out the seven-card Wisdom Reading. Life came up in the Positive position followed by Duality in the Negative. That was tricky. Then, from bottom to top, we got Loyalty, Mind, Courage and Spirit. The final card in the Teacher position was Love.

This was not a happy reading. On the surface it all looked good. Except for that Duality card in the negative position. That meant all the other cards could represent their opposite quality. This didn't say much good for Patrice Kirkwood or Miss Reynolds.

The next week was a frenzy. It was full-on Christmas season now. I had been selected to sing *Silent Night* at the school pageant and had to practice after school. J. Dyanne and I consulted the Wisdom Cards and practiced stillness every day, but neither of us got much, just a jumble of tangled emotions and images.

After J. Dyanne developed and examined the photos from Weaver's office, she saw that though they looked clean with a cursory scan, upon closer study it was clear the math didn't add up. Trust J. Dyanne to figure that out.

Dad had spoken with Mr. Sadowski who confirmed that his company used to be on the shelter project and he had been pretty upset about losing it to Reynolds. He had then landed a bigger contract with the city, and so he wasn't worried much about losing the smaller job. Alderman Weaver was covering his tracks. The good news was that Dad was going to get some work on the city contract with Sadowski.

Mom mentioned that Weaver was going to support Rev. Ingle in setting up a federally funded school lunch program to support our neighborhood school, Harvard Elementary. It was situated right across the street from the church, so Rev. Ingle was happy to support the idea of hosting the program, but he was now cautious about working with the alderman. He didn't want to get involved in any misuse of federal funds. And Teri Brinker was calling about the big scoop J. Dyanne had promised. She was certainly tenacious.

J. Dyanne was confident that something would break. She had Derek following Miss Reynolds in case Patrice was actually plotting to put her in a cage. The only thing he had to report so far was that Miss Reynolds was bringing home a lot of empty boxes. Maybe she was sending out a lot of Christmas packages.

We were a week away from Christmas break. J. Dyanne, Derek and I were again on the church program assembly line at Mom's office when Rev. Ingle arrived. He looked pretty somber.

"It looks like I'll need to re-write my sermon for tomorrow." Mom wasn't so happy about that. She'd just finished typing the other one. Rev. Ingle turned to J. Dyanne.

"It seems your suspicions were correct about Alderman Weaver."

"You found proof?" I asked.

"The proof found me. I received a letter from Dolores Reynolds."

"She confessed?" Derek blurted out.

"In a manner of speaking. She's written to me in the hope that I could initiate a formal investigation into Weaver's misappropriation of public funds. She mentions you." He turned to J. Dyanne and began to read. *"'Miss Dubois only uncovered half the story. Perhaps she can assist in uncovering the rest.'"* He handed J. Dyanne the letter.

"She thinks highly of you--" Ingle stopped speaking and stared. With good reason.

J. Dyanne had become rigid, and then began to violently shake. Her hands clutched the letter, her eyes clamped shut. Mom rushed to her and ripped the letter from her hands. The result was immediate – the seizure stopped – Mom caught her as J. Dyanne slumped forward. She then reached up and caught Mom's sweater, gasping.

"She's not crying anymore. But she hurts. She wants to hurt. Got to find her. It's bad. It's really bad."

"What is she talking about?"

"Miss Reynolds. Something's wrong with Miss Reynolds." I was sure this is what J. Dyanne meant.

"That letter, Miss Reynolds wrote it. Her feelings... sometimes when Dyanne touches things she can tell... she sees what's happening with whoever the thing belongs to."

There was no doubt in Rev. Ingle's mind now. He was a believer.

"Okay. Then if Miss Reynolds needs help we'll find her."

"I know where she lives," Derek offered. "We can go over there."

"All right, son. You lead the way."

J. Dyanne struggled to get up.

"I've got to go..." But Mom wasn't having it.

"You will stay where you are. You too, Katrin. They can check on that girl and let us know." I knew that tone from *mater familias*, and so I didn't argue. Mom sat J. Dyanne down in one of the office chairs.

"I'm going down to the kitchen and get you something warm to drink. If either one of you moves before I get back..." She didn't have to finish the sentence. The warning was more than clear.

We were exactly where Mom left us when she returned with two cups of hot chocolate.

"Don't speak until you finish," she ordered. Again, we obeyed. Mom started collating, stapling and folding the church programs with a deathly quiet efficiency. How she knew we had finished when she hadn't once glanced in our direction, I'm not quite sure. But we had just swallowed the last dregs of chocolate when she turned to us. Her face had softened in a way I'd never seen before. There was... I can only think of one word that described what I saw in her eyes. Sorrow. She looked straight at J. Dyanne.

"I didn't want this for you," she began. "It's hard for me to watch you take on this kind of responsibility." Frustrated, she turned back to collating the programs. "You're not even in high school yet."

I could tell that Mom was mixing up the pages. So could J. Dyanne. We got up, took the mismatched pages from her and fixed them. Mom watched us for a moment and then started collating again.

"You two are stronger than I was at your age. Tougher. I guess you have to be these days."

We continued the rest of the work in silence.

* * *

That evening, as promised, we let Dad know we were planning to make our move on Alderman Weaver. We had a plan worked out with Rev. Ingle that would, hopefully, unfold perfectly at church. To our surprise Dad said he would be there. He'd only come to church on one other occasion – to hear us sing in the choir last Easter.

The news that Dolores Reynolds was missing in action was of some concern. Her apartment had been found spotless and still. All of her belongings had been packed in the boxes she had collected and were neatly stacked and labeled in the living room.

Rev. Ingle had already invited Alderman Weaver to the service because his previous plan was to announce the opening of the new school lunch program to the congregation. He didn't rescind the invite, and Alderman Weaver was sure to be there. Shrewd politician that he was, he knew a good photo opportunity when he saw one.

J. Dyanne put in the call to Teri Brinker, inviting her to attend church the next day. Ten o'clock service. The cameraman would need to wait outside, but he should be ready to roll at a moment's notice.

# Chapter 28 - Sanctuary

"The topic of today's sermon is Deception," began Rev. Ingle. "'Oh what a tangled web we weave, when first we practice to deceive.' I know you've heard that before. I believe it was Mr. Shakespeare who wrote that."

"Sir Walter Scott," I groaned. J. Dyanne nudged me to be quiet. Derek smirked. We were seated just behind Alderman Weaver in the second row. Patrice and her friend Audrey were on the other side of the aisle. I couldn't believe Patrice had the nerve to come to church. Dad was sitting in the back row and Teri Brinker sat opposite. She wanted a clear view of everything. There was still no sign of Miss Reynolds.

"This quotation speaks to the consequences of the web weaver," Ingle continued. "But what of the one who is deceived? Are they condemned to suffer forever for falling under the spell of the serpent, just as Eve was so deceived in the garden? Or can such a person be redeemed?"

He set his piercing gaze straight at Patrice. She shifted in her seat.

"Time will surely tell." His gaze swept the congregation. I was getting that antsy feeling again. Rev. Ingle liked the spotlight and I didn't want him to get carried away with his oratory. I got still and connected, concentrating on 'get to the point' vibes.

"This morning I had planned to acknowledge someone for organizing a new community program. But then I received a communication from a parishioner. You all know Miss Dolores Reynolds. What you may not know is that Miss Reynolds has been missing these past two days. You may also have heard that she was involved in some questionable financial activity while employed with Alderman Weaver. The Alderman had no choice but to dismiss her, but he supported her in finding work at the Auburn Park Shelter and Food Center."

There were nods of approval from some in the congregation. Weaver graciously accepted the approval.

"But I have fears for Miss Reynolds," Rev. Ingle continued, "because it was to me, her pastor, to whom she sent this letter; a letter to untangle a web of deception; a tangled web wrought... by Alderman Weaver."

The congregation fell silent. And then Miss Reynolds walked into the sanctuary. All heads turned as she walked to the front pew and took a seat. Warren Murphy, Weaver's driver, followed and sat behind her. He gave Weaver a warning glance.

I felt J. Dyanne stiffen next to me. Rev. Ingle

looked surprised, as did Weaver. I could hear Teri Brinker feverishly scribbling on her notepad.

"Dyanne? What's wrong?" J. Dyanne looked like she did when she first touched Reynolds' letter.

"Reynolds. She's not well." J. Dyanne looked over at Reynolds and Warren. "This is not good." I tried to give Rev. Ingle a signal, but he was into it now.

"Let me read from this letter. *'Dear Pastor, I know I have done wrong, but it was out of love. But I see now that I was deceived. I was used. My love and my loyalty were used by a man I trusted to have my best interests in his heart. But it is clear that he only serves his own. I tell you this that others will not fall under his spell. It may be too late for me, but Patrice Kirkwood is only seventeen. It might not be too late for her.'*" Naturally, Patrice could not be silent.

"She's lying. She's crazy!" Patrice shrieked. That's when, as they say, all hell broke loose.

Alderman Weaver stood up and advanced toward the pulpit, demanding that Rev. Ingle stop reading the lies of a mentally damaged woman. Patrice continued screeching about the accusations against her, stalking toward Miss Reynolds.

"Stay away," Reynolds warned. But Patrice continued to advance. Reynolds reached into her purse, but before she could do anything, Warren grabbed her arm, twisting it down. Reynolds struggled and screamed.

"Don't! Let me go!" Warren was having a time with her. As she tried to pull away, the flash of a blade sparked in the light streaming from the stained glass windows.

And then J. Dyanne pushed free from the cover of Mom's arm and raced forward.

"Dolores! Stop! Don't move. Just... be still!"

Miss Reynolds wasn't the only one surprised. The congregation was riveted. I didn't know what J. Dyanne was talking about. But Miss Reynolds did what J. Dyanne asked. Warren had pulled Reynolds' arm behind her back. J. Dyanne stared him down.

"It's not going to work," she said. "Let her go."

"She's dangerous. She's got a knife," Warren blustered.

"No she doesn't. It's your knife."

Miss Reynolds took advantage of Warren's surprise and broke free. Again, the sunlight flashed on the blade, sending slivers of light winking throughout the sanctuary as the knife fell from Warren's grasp.

"He tried to kill me!" Reynolds shouted. Rev. Ingle came forward and led Miss Reynolds away.

"That's hers," Warren insisted. "You saw her reach for it. I took it from her." He looked to Alderman Weaver for corroboration. But if he expected Weaver to back him up, he was mistaken. No politician wanted any part of this.

J. Dyanne picked up Miss Reynolds' purse. In it were a package of tissue and a small can of mace.

"I was getting my spray," Miss Reynolds insisted. "That girl was coming after me. I was gonna spray her, that's all."

Warren backed away. But he didn't get far. Teri Brinker had already signaled her crew. Warren ran right into the glare of the cameraman's spotlight. It was time for his fifteen minutes of fame.

## Chapter 29 - Solstice

Afterward, several people swore they saw J. Dyanne shoot sparks of fire through the air, forcing Warren to drop the knife. It didn't help that Miss Reynolds fervently told anyone who would listen that J. Dyanne's voice had cut through her like ice, freezing her on the spot like the command of an avenging angel. Well, what can you expect? It happened in a church, after all. Belief is truth as far as that goes.

Miss Reynolds insisted that if she had kept struggling, Warren Murphy would have cut her and made it seem like self-defense. When questioned about the mace, Miss Reynolds explained that once she decided to expose Alderman Weaver, she knew she had to protect herself.

It was a tangled web indeed. I had no idea how J. Dyanne knew what Warren was up to. She explained it all for Brinker's benefit, off-camera of course.

The fact that Miss Reynolds would take the fall for skimming the petty cash clearly spoke to a more intimate relationship with the Alderman.

But Weaver also had his eye on Patrice, who at

seventeen was still too young, but had potential. He convinced her that she would be a perfect politician's wife, once she turned eighteen. With this in mind, Weaver had secured the community service position for Patrice at the food center, rather than any formal charges being laid against her. And when he needed a position for Miss Reynolds after her firing, Patrice was more than happy to help him by framing Morton. It was her idea to kill two birds with one stone that led her to try and frame J. Dyanne, too.

But Patrice made the mistake of bragging to Miss Reynolds about Weaver's involvement in keeping her out of juvenile detention and their long-term marriage plans. This just pushed Reynolds over the edge. You know what they say about a woman scorned. And no, that's not from Shakespeare, either.

All of this web weaving was supported by Weaver's right-hand, fix-it man, Warren Murphy. Once Miss Reynolds became a loose emotional cannon, she needed to be handled or their money train would derail. Warren saw an opportunity to manipulate a self-defense encounter to cover what could have been the permanent silencing of a liability.

After the story broke, Miss Reynolds moved down south to be with her father's people. The Kirkwoods finally took control of their daughter and sent her to a Catholic boarding school. Teri Brinker was thrilled with the story and kept her promise to keep J. Dyanne's name out of her reports. But that didn't stop the neighborhood rumors.

Alderman Weaver refused to resign but he certainly wasn't going to be reelected. The petition for his recall was moving along very well. And the best part was that he'd totally burned out his talents. Fear is a powerful thing.

* * *

Grand Anne was very proud of how things turned out. But of course she didn't tell us that. There was still work to be done. We knew she and Great Aunt Alis were pleased though because they invited J. Dyanne and me on an excursion to the Loop to see the department store Christmas window decorations. It was the day of the winter solstice. We watched the successful Apollo 8 liftoff that morning. And not just for school. It really was an amazing sight. The sun was shining and we were out of school until after the New Year. What could be better?

Despite the cold of Chicago's wind chill factor, we joined the crowds of onlookers, moving from window to window of Marshall Field's. Each window told a story with moving toys, dolls and fake, sparkly snow. We then went over to my favorite place, the Central Library.

It was magnificent, as usual. And warm. We walked up the marble staircase to the general delivery room where you could ask for books from deep within the stacks of the library. This was my favorite room. Up above was a most magnificent dome.

"This is the largest Tiffany glass dome in the world," J. Dyanne informed us. Of course, she would know this obscure fact.

"It's like the dome in the Wisdom Cards," I said.

"The dome in the Wisdom Cards," Grand Anne explained, "symbolizes the rising sun of unity awareness. And here, it's like the dome of the illumined sky."

I turned in a circle to read the quotation encircling the base of the dome: *"'Books are the legacies that a great genius leaves to mankind, which are delivered down from generation to generation as presents to the posterity of those who are yet unborn.'"* I looked to Grand Anne. "Are we getting books today?"

"Oh yes," said Grand Anne. "Your studies have barely begun." Aunt Alis was still looking up at the dome.

"You should have seen it before they put the concrete on the outside," she said. "These electric lights just don't do it justice."

"Why would they do that?"

"Some people just don't like too much light," she responded.

"The oculus shows the twelve signs of the zodiac, representing navigation and exploration," Grand Anne pointed out. The symbols were barely visible, and though it was still beautiful, it was kind of dark.

"What did it look like before?" J. Dyanne asked. Alis and Grand Anne looked at each other, a secret smile shared between them.

"What time is it?"

"Just before one."

"Jacqueléne. Can you tell us what 'solstice' means?" J. Dyanne looked at Grand Anne and then at Aunt Alis, with just a hint of suspicion in her eyes.

"We're not here by accident, are we?"

"You got that right, girly," Aunt Alis grinned. "Now, just answer the question."

"Solstice is a combination of *sol,* the sun and *sistere,* to stand still. At the solstice, the movement of the sun appears to come to a standstill."

"Give me your hand. It's time," said Grand Anne.

We each linked hands under the dome. Grand Anne began to speak.

"The solstice, the time the sun stands still, is an auspicious time for us to also be still," said Grand Anne. And then, as we stood, her musical voice described the luminescence of the dome.

"At its creation, when the solstice sun shone through the colored glass, all things, both animate and inanimate, became suffused with a rose gold light. It glistened on the marble and sparked the gilded framework to fire." In that moment I no longer needed imagination. It was as if the dome of the library blossomed to life. Transcendent light streamed throughout the room. I could see the full spectrum raining down in sparkling columns, pouring into each of us until we were all shimmering bodies of light.

It glowed brilliant for one breathless moment. Then the heavens moved and the world settled down to normal.

## Affinity

August 1971

From that day forward there was a new definition of 'normal' in our lives. On the surface, our world was still familiar. For instance, that day at the Central Library with Grand Anne we checked out books as usual. However, they were not our usual mystery and detective novels. We were taken to a section we'd never entered before and took out books on psychical research, mediums and telepathy.

Over the holidays, J. Dyanne continued to create art but she'd moved away from paint-by-number sets to pencil drawings depicting scenes from our recent adventures. My favorite was of Derek, J. Dyanne and me in the shelter while she conversed with Emmitt's spirit. She also drew her own version of Apollo 8's image of Earthrise. J. Dyanne said the half dome of the planet, glowing within the vast expanse of space was similar to her own mindscape when her talents were active. A perspective was rising on the inside, just as it was on the outside.

For me, normal meant holding on to our Christmas traditions. After all we'd been through,

I wanted Christmas to just be Christmas. The talisman Grand Anne had given me at Thanksgiving felt like just a pretty necklace lately. So I relaxed into the festivities: the candlelight service on Christmas Eve, Mom's excellent cooking, stringing popcorn for the tree, eggnog, memorizing *Twas the Night Before Christmas* and best of all... the lights. And not just on the tree. Outside, our block was the best-lit street in the entire neighborhood. The Winthrop Block Association decreed that each house would have a string of multicolored lights that stretched from the house to the tree in each front yard, plus lights around our front windows. And when it snowed, it was a wonderland.

I didn't even mind Derek's more frequent visits to our house. He thought he was a pool shark, but unlike the Female Teen Elder who would play badly on purpose so the boys would win, I regularly beat Derek at eight ball. Besides, even if he was my boyfriend, and he definitely wasn't, I still wouldn't fake playing badly just so he could feel superior. If that's what it took to get a boyfriend, I guess I'd never have one. Dad understood, and agreed with me.

Even putting up with the terrible twins, Darla and Darlene on Christmas Eve was good, because it was normal. You could count on them to get into something and they didn't disappoint. This year they 'accidentally' opened half the presents under the tree.

Mid-week between Christmas and New Year's,

Aunt Gina had her annual holiday feast at her apartment in the projects. Though typically freezing outside, the apartment was always so hot we had to have the window open.

Again, it was familiar but different. I could see how Aunt Velma kept her eyes on J. Dyanne, once again pulling me aside to ask if I was looking out for her. This time she focused her unsteady gaze at the pendant Grand Anne had given me.

"Oh, so you got it," she whispered. "Good. That's good."

That started me wondering if Aunt Velma was more than just a relative, too. I took a long look at my extended family this year. Who were they really? And exactly where did J. Dyanne and I fit in?

Apparently, *mater* and *pater familias* had some talent. But why did Mom not want this life for us? And the Teen Elder Others, did they have talent? And what about the cousins on both sides... did they know? As the days of 1968 dwindled down I let those questions diminish. New Year's Eve was upon us.

You know, at the start of these chronicles I stated how I always had high hopes for August, a time of anticipation for something to happen that would make a summer memory to last a lifetime. Well, that certainly occurred, even more than I bargained for. It was now the winter version of those summer days of promise.

Usually there was eagerness for a grand finale to complete the year. But it was different now.

For me it wasn't about an ending. It was anticipation for the new beginning. Just like the Apollo 8 astronauts said from space on Christmas Eve. At the approaching lunar sunrise, they read from the book of Genesis: "*In the beginning...*"

Well, here on earth at 7541 Winthrop, we were most definitely at the start of a new beginning. A way of being that not everyone would understand. And some would fear.

My goal in writing these chronicles is so you will not be swayed by the rumors concerning the path we've undertaken. This is, indeed, the true canon of Jacqueléne Dyanne DuBois.

And remember what Grand Anne says: "*If you don't write your own history, someone else will make it up for you.*" I'd listen to her, if I were you.

**End of**
**Volume 1**

# Author's Note

When looking at the past what often comes to mind are the highlights — personal ones, as well as those considered historical.

When I look back at my own childhood the historical highlights run side by side with vibrant personal memories. Such a memory was the spark for "Katrin's Chronicles: The Canon of Jacqueléne Dyanne, Vol. 1."

This favored recollection happened more than forty years ago. It was one of those magical summer vacation days on the South Side of Chicago and my elder sister decided we would go on an adventure. She packed provisions in a brown paper lunch bag and proceeded to lead me on a trek to distant lands. Under her direction and narration our neighborhood street became an alluring foreign metropolis. The vacant lot transformed from a wasteland of overgrown weeds sprouting throughout the concrete remains of a demolished building into a lush jungle, and then a desert where we found an oasis in which to rest and consume our rations.

Yes, in the broader spectrum of 1968 the world was experiencing mammoth shifts of social consciousness. And yet amidst the turmoil, it was still possible for two young girls to thrive and relish a life of imagination. And it was perhaps critical that they did so. Transformation is never easy, for individuals or society. It can begin subtly and then, as it progresses, it often becomes turbulent, violent and frightening, with moments of calm, assured grace, mystery and beauty.

There is never just one side to the story of history. It's not to say news reports and history books are wrong. It's just not the full story. And how could it be? We may all live on the same planet, but we each experience and interpret the shared events of the world through our own personal lens. The facts are straightforward and simple. The history — depending on who tells the story — is fascinating.

"Katrin's Chronicles: The Canon of Jacqueléne Dyanne, Vol. 1." is a work of fiction, for the most part. Though not comprehensive by any means, the following pages list some of the historical events that reverberated in the young lives of Katrin and J. Dyanne.

# Historical Events of 1968 Summary

Protests and demonstrations were ever-present throughout the United States and around the world. The primary topics in the U.S. were as follows:

**Vietnam War:** The over-riding topic of news at this time was the escalating U.S. military involvement in the on-going conflict between North and South Vietnam. By 1968 there were over 500,000 U.S. troops deployed in Southeast Asia. For the first time in history, technological advances brought video footage from the front lines into the living rooms of America on a daily basis. Never before had the brutality of war been televised on such a broad scale. This caused many Americans, especially young adults, to protest against the war.

**Civil Rights Movement and the Black Power Movement:** The non-violent protests of the late 1950's and early 1960's brought about a number of changes toward equal opportunity for Black Americans. However, the fight for racial equality was far from over. By 1968 an outgrowth of the Civil Rights Movement was the Black Power Movement, which advocated self-determination, racial pride and community socio-economic power and freedom.

**Women's Liberation Movement:** What has come to be known as "second wave feminism" was shifting the social and cultural role of women around the nation and the world. Women were demanding equal opportunities in all areas of society and the workforce, traditionally dominated by men. For example, in 1968 women were still excluded from such Ivy League universities as Yale, Princeton and

Dartmouth. Harvard had its "sister" college, Radcliffe.

**Politics:** 1968 was a national election year. With all the social and cultural upheaval, tensions within the political sphere were heightened. When President Lyndon Johnson announced during his Address to the Nation in March that he would neither seek nor accept a nomination for re-election in the coming election, it shifted everything in the political arena.

# 1968 Timeline

**April 4**
Civil Rights leader, Rev. Dr. Martin Luther King, Jr. was staying at the Lorraine Motel in Memphis, Tennessee where he was planning the Poor People's March on Washington. While standing on a balcony greeting friends in the motel courtyard, Dr. King was shot by a sniper. An hour later he was declared dead. The assassination sparked rioting across the country.

**June 5 - 6**
U.S. Senator and Presidential candidate Robert F. Kennedy addressed supporters at the Ambassador Hotel in Los Angeles after winning the California Democratic presidential primary. Following his address Kennedy left the stage, and while being escorted through the hotel kitchen, he was shot. His assailant was captured on the scene. Senator Kennedy, brother of assassinated President John F. Kennedy, died from his wounds the following day.

**August 26 - 29**
The City of Chicago, led by Mayor Richard J. Daley, hosted The Democratic National Convention at the International Amphitheatre. The nominations for president and vice president went to then Vice President Hubert J. Humphrey and Senator Edmund S. Muskie of Maine, respectively.

In a year of national unrest and turmoil, over 10,000 demonstrators gathered in the streets of downtown Chicago during the four days of the Convention. This prompted the mayor to bring out the Illinois National Guard to supplement the Chicago Police Department for a total security force of over 23,000. On August 28th clashes between demonstrators and police escalated, with marchers beaten unconscious, over 100 others sent to emergency rooms and 175 arrested. All was shown live on national television, while demonstrators chanted "The whole world is watching." Even network news anchors inside the Convention Hall were roughed up by security.

**September 7**
Feminists, led by The New York Radical Women and joined by members of the National Organization for Women, disrupted the Miss America Beauty Contest in Atlantic City, New Jersey, by unfurling a banner in the auditorium during the live broadcast that read "Women's Liberation." In one of the first national demonstrations to promote women's liberation, nearly 400 women also marched on the Atlantic City Boardwalk and dumped female-centered items into a "Freedom Trash Can," including bras, curlers, pots and pans and girdles. Though nothing was actually burned, the media dubbed them "bra-burning feminists," likely linking them to anti-war protesters who burned draft cards.

**October 11**
NASA launched Apollo 7, the first manned mission in the Apollo space program, with astronauts Wally Schirra, Donn Eisele and Walter Cunningham. This mission had the first live television broadcast from orbit and tested the lunar module docking maneuver in preparation for a planned moon landing.

**October 12 - 27**
The Games of the XIX Olympiad, more commonly known as The Summer Olympic Games, were held in Mexico City. As with most events during this chaotic year, the Games had their own controversies. Boycotts were threatened if apartheid South Africa participated. U.S. athletes Tommie Smith and John Carlos lowered their heads, and raised black-gloved hands fisted in a Black Power salute during their medal ceremony for winning the gold and bronze in the 200-meter dash. They were suspended from the U.S. team and banned from the Olympic Village.

**November 5**
U.S. Election Day. Republican Richard M. Nixon won the presidency with 43.4 percent of the popular vote. Democrat Hubert Humphrey garnered 42.7 percent and George Wallace received 13.5 percent with 0.4 percent for other candidates.

**December 21**
NASA launched Apollo 8, the first manned spacecraft to leave Earth's orbit. It was also the first manned United States mission to orbit the Moon. Astronauts Frank Borman, Jim Lovell and William A. Anders were the first humans to see the far side of the Moon, as well as Earth in its entirety.

**December 24**
On Christmas Eve, the astronauts of Apollo 8 read the first 10 verses from the Book of Genesis while orbiting the Moon. This was the most-watched broadcast of the time. The crew transmitted the iconic color image of our planet, known as "Earthrise."

***Discover more about the world of Katrin and J. Dyanne at: www.jdyanne.com.***

# Acknowledgments

The encouragement, thoughtful advice and support of many people helped to make this book a reality. It all begins with my family who nurtured, teased, taught, loved and created such vibrant memories that provided the inspiration for these stories.

Thank you to the reader friends who applauded the birth of these stories: Sabrina, Margaret, Karin, Leonard, Frauke, Chris, Alastair, Phylicia, Mickie Landol, Clyde Fontenette, Samantha Brewer, Olivia Haynes and so many more. Your enthusiasm to keep reading kept me writing.

Thank you to my fellow writing friends for your sharp eye for grammar, continuity, history and structure: Glenn Berenbeim, DeeAnn Veeder, David Man, Barri Clark, and Sherli Evans.

Many thanks to Kate Hewett for her artistry and patience with this author as you created the cover art.

Shari Goodhartz, you are a boon to the endeavors of this author/publisher. I value your friendship and your editing expertise.

And thanks to J.D. Woods Consulting for not just the book design, but especially for your persistent faith in this story and my writing.

I also gratefully acknowledge the support, encouragement and creative forum provided by Jill Schary Robinson and the Wimpole Street Writers Group (and of course, all the delicious dinners). (www.wimpolestreetwriters.com)

# About the Author

Valerie C. Woods is the author of the novella ***I Believe... A Ghost Story for the Holidays.***

She also wrote ***Something for Everyone (50 Original Monologues),*** offered by renowned play publishers, Samuel French, Inc.

Ms. Woods continues to write for the entertainment industry. Her career began with her selection as a Walt Disney Screenwriting Fellow and continued with writing and producing for such network and cable dramas as *Under One Roof, Touched By An Angel, Promised Land, Any Day Now* and *Soul Food.* She has returned to her first love... writing fiction, in addition to developing future film and television projects.

**Learn more about the author at: www.ValerieCWoods.com**

Coming in 2014

Volume 2
of
Katrin's Chronicles:

Jacqueléne Dyanne
and
The Scrying Bowl

Valerie C. Woods

Made in the USA
San Bernardino, CA
10 November 2013